Addy's Eyes Drifted Open Slowly

Spenser was crouched at her side, fingers tangled in her hair. She felt a physical click run through her system as his gaze locked with hers, bringing her closer to wakefulness.

"You know, you're incredibly beautiful when you sleep." His voice was soft and low. She opened her mouth in surprise and he immediately covered it with his own. Someone was moaning softly. Addy was afraid it was her. Her brain struggled to recall how she'd gotten into this situation.

Spenser had been explaining something about the will, the house and the money.... His teeth nipped at her lower lip and he pulled her closer. *Something about living here for six months...*but there was more, she was sure of it....

With a near shriek of rage, Addy tore her mouth from Spenser's and shoved hard at his shoulders.

"Did you say that I have to be married?"

Dear Reader,

Thank you for choosing Silhouette Desire. As always, we have a fabulous array of stories for you to enjoy, starting with *Just a Taste* by Bronwyn Jameson, the latest installment in our DYNASTIES: THE ASHTONS continuity series. This tale of forbidden attraction between two romance-wary souls will leave you breathless and wanting more from this wonderful author—who will have a brand-new miniseries of her own, PRINCES OF THE OUTBACK, out later this year.

The terrific Annette Broadrick is back with another book in her CRENSHAWS OF TEXAS series. *Double Identity* is an engrossing page-turner about seduction and lies…you know, all that good stuff! Susan Crosby continues her BEHIND CLOSED DOORS series with *Rules of Attraction*, the first of three brand-new stories set in the world of very private investigations. Roxanne St. Claire brings us a fabulous McGrath brother hero caught in an unexpected situation, in *When the Earth Moves*. Rochelle Alers's THE BLACKSTONES OF VIRGINIA series wraps up with *Beyond Business*, a story in which the Blackstone patriarch gets involved in a surprise romance with his new—and very pregnant—assistant. And last but certainly not least, the engaging Amy Jo Cousins is back this month with *Sleeping Arrangements*, a terms-of-the-will story not to be missed.

Here's hoping you enjoy all six of our selections this month. And, in the months to come, look for Maureen Child's THREE-WAY WAGER series and a brand-new installment of our infamous TEXAS CATTLEMAN'S CLUB.

Happy reading!

Melissa Jeglinski

Melissa Jeglinski
Senior Editor
Silhouette Desire

Please address questions and book requests to:
Silhouette Reader Service
U.S.: 3010 Walden Ave., P.O. Box 1325, Buffalo, NY 14269
Canadian: P.O. Box 609, Fort Erie, Ont. L2A 5X3

Sleeping
ARRANGEMENTS

AMY JO COUSINS

Published by Silhouette Books
America's Publisher of Contemporary Romance

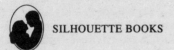

SILHOUETTE BOOKS

ISBN 0-373-76650-5

SLEEPING ARRANGEMENTS

Copyright © 2005 by Amy Jo Albinack

Visit Silhouette Books at www.eHarlequin.com

Printed in U.S.A.

Books by Amy Jo Cousins

Silhouette Desire

At Your Service #1560
Sleeping Arrangements #1650

AMY JO COUSINS

loves words of all kinds, and her love of reading naturally led to a love of writing. Amy also has a passion for languages and there's nothing she likes better than learning a new language and using it to explore the history of a foreign country, whether standing on the beaches of D-Day in Normandy or outside the Olympic Stadium in Munich.

Her collection of books is slowly crowding her out of her home, although her cat seems more than willing to fall asleep upon the various piles. Other than that, Amy loves learning how to do anything that takes her outdoors and away from her computer including kayaking, sculling, rock climbing and landscape water painting.

For the Albinack boys—
Bruce Edward, Matthew McKinley and Finley Edward.
You set the bar high, fellas.

One

"**I** admit I didn't expect a professional appearance, but I thought at least you'd be clean."

The crisp voice crawled like ice down Addy's spine, drawing her up straighter with each word. Pride and irritation kept her from turning around to respond to the man who'd walked into the law office behind her.

She brushed a hand reflexively over her filthy blue jeans. No sense even trying to straighten her ratty curls. Running her fingers through her hair wouldn't remove the caked mud, although, according to the mirror in her pickup truck, she was fairly sure she'd managed to pick out all of the twigs. The rest of her muck-covered body was definitely a lost cause.

"I told your assistant this was a bad time for me, but she insisted this was the only appointment you had available."

Sharp footsteps on the worn linoleum floor allowed her to pull her body to the side, avoiding the man's passing. As he moved to stand behind the scarred wood desk, she got her first glimpse of the man who'd been leaving increasingly irritated messages on her answering machine over the last month.

She wondered if Mr. Spencer Reed ever cut himself on the sharp creases in his pants. Certainly the suit he wore as if it had been hand sewn for him by a London tailor was worth more than her entire wardrobe. Even his horn-rimmed glasses looked more stylish than anything she'd ever owned. Ignoring the demon in her mind that whispered of a blond Christopher Reeve in Clark Kent mode, she let her gaze roam casually over his face and body in a manner calculated to return insult.

Dark blond hair waving in deliberately casual disarray indicated an excellent barber. His cheekbones screamed good breeding, and that firm mouth surely never uttered words unless it was to bend courts and clients to his will. The emotionless ice-blue gaze made it difficult to look away. She reminded herself that she'd always found her family's uniformly dark eyes to be warm and welcoming. This man, she thought, was easily summed up by a few of her least favorite words.

Slick. Cultured. Upper-class.

Because she couldn't stomach hypocrisy, even her own, she admitted that a couple more words could be added to that list. Compelling. Coolly handsome. The seduction of assurance. If he bothered to turn on the charm, she'd probably be a lost cause.

The mismatch of his appearance with the ratty look of his office momentarily sparked her curiosity. Mr. Sharp-Dressed Man just didn't fit in with these worn and tatty surroundings. She forced herself to ignore the temptation to speculate on his circumstances.

The trust fund on legs was still speaking. She dragged her attention back, annoyed further that he seemed to take no notice of her rudeness.

"I am very busy, and most people find ten o'clock to be a perfectly civilized hour for a business meeting."

"I'm not most people."

"Clearly."

Addy kept a throttling grip on her temper. She wished she possessed the same control over the flush she felt heating up her cheeks. Her awareness of being inappropriately dressed combined with his implication that his time was far more valuable than hers had kindled a fire of embarrassment and anger that she knew he read on her face.

"Listen, Mr. Reed. You called. I came. What's so important I had to interrupt my job for you?"

"Your job. Would that be ladies' mud wrestling?"

Her vision blurred. Addy was dimly aware that she might have spit at him in her struggle to get the sharp-edged words out fast enough. She glanced at his stunned silence then grabbed the closest solid object. Only his quick grip on her arm stopped her from pitching his etched-marble nameplate at his elegant face.

"I'm sorry." The words took a long moment to penetrate the haze of her anger. "I'm sorry. That was completely uncalled for and very unprofessional. I've had a long, frustrating morning, but that is no excuse for taking out my bad temper on you. Can we begin again? I'm Spencer Reed. Would you care for a cup of coffee?"

His outstretched hand across the desk was meant as a peace offering, she supposed. And the lopsided grin was meant to be soothing. She managed to keep her mouth shut, but enjoyed thinking about where he could stick his charm.

"Save it for someone you can still make a good impression on," she snapped. "What do you want?"

He sighed and eyed her briefly over the tops of his glasses, as if debating whether to continue his apologies. She caught herself before she could ask him to take the glasses off so she could see if he looked as good without them as he did with them on. After a moment, he shrugged and lifted a stack of legal documents off the corner of his desk. With a gesture, he indicated the armchair facing the desk.

Addy shook her head. Whatever business he had with her, she preferred to hear it standing. Getting cozy was not an option.

"I hope I'm not the bearer of bad news," he said slowly. "Last month Mrs. Adeline O'Connell passed away in her sleep."

A glancing wave of shock made her falter for a moment. Although she'd not seen the woman since she was a baby, Addy was her great-aunt's namesake. She hadn't known of her death. Carefully schooling her face to blankness, she replied briskly.

"My condolences to her family."

"You are her family." The stern look he shot at her felt like a scolding.

"Mr. Reed, the last time I saw my great-aunt, I was in diapers. I haven't heard from her since, and I certainly don't consider her a part of my family." She clipped the words out as she glanced at the men's watch on her wrist. There was still time to return to her crew and try to clean up the disaster she'd left behind at the construction site.

"Perhaps you don't. However, Mrs. O'Connell apparently considered you a part of hers. The reading of her will took place immediately after her funeral, and she has left you a significant bequest."

With one hand, he plucked a document off the top of his stack and placed it on the desk in front of her.

"Is that what this is all about?" Her astonished laugh echoed in the sparsely furnished room. "I could have saved us both a lot of trouble if you'd bothered to mention that in your messages." She pushed the papers right back at him. "I'm not interested in anything that woman wanted to give me."

"Don't be too hasty, Ms. Tyler. Think of it as your Free Parking jackpot."

It took her a moment to place the Monopoly reference.

"Oh, shut up." The words she'd repressed at the mention of Adeline O'Connell burst out of her like an erupting volcano. "That woman treated my mother like dirt her entire life. She took pleasure in hurting people. Took pleasure in trying to make people feel ashamed of themselves." She grabbed her backpack from the floor, where she'd originally dropped it. "I wouldn't take anything of hers if you plated it in gold and tied it up with a pink ribbon. Thanks, but no thanks. I'm out of here."

She swung the heavy pack on her shoulder and whirled to stalk out the office door. His footsteps followed hers more quickly than she would have expected.

"Ms. Tyler." Her name in his mouth rang with the command of an order to halt and his palm smacked against the door, holding it shut. She stopped with her hand on the knob, but refused to turn and face him. "There is a monetary bequest of nearly fifty thousand dollars, and also a property."

These words did move her.

He was so close that her shoulder brushed against him as she turned. She was shorter, and resented having to look up at him. She also resented that being this close to him, closer than was comfortable, and knowing that his hand held the door shut behind her, was making her pulse race. She was dancing on a thin line between dislike and desire.

"Don't insult me." She let the words drop like individual stones into a still lake. "Your apology was not accepted and neither is hers. Not everyone can be bought."

His lake-blue eyes narrowed and dropped as he tilted his head a little bit.

"You know, when you're not behaving with all the polish of a truck driver," he said after a moment, "you are quite unfairly beautiful."

She pulled her shoulders back and turned her face away from him, all of a sudden sure that he would kiss her in a moment if she didn't move. They stood frozen for silent seconds. She felt more than heard him exhale and realized she was holding her own breath as he dropped his hand from the door.

The moment had passed, which allowed her to face him again.

"Don't fool yourself, Counselor. I'm not for sale."

With those words, she yanked the door open and slammed

it behind her. The resounding crash she left in her wake was the most satisfying moment of her morning.

She would have been even more pleased if she'd managed to shut the door before his parting shot chased after her.

"Everyone is for sale, Ms. Tyler, in my experience. Particularly women."

In the parking lot outside the nondescript office building, she cranked the key in the ignition and pulled onto the street, tires squealing in sympathetic anger. She took the corners tightly and the straightaways at speed, with two monologues battling in her head. Her conscious mind bowed to her will, focusing on the difficulties she'd faced this morning with the clearly inaccurate geographic survey of her latest engineering project. The shopping center was a tricky design, involving floodplain issues that demanded absolute accuracy. Repeated problems had forced her to the drastic step of going out to the site herself with the surveyors and wading through the January snowdrifts. A heretofore unrecorded runoff stream, hidden under layers of Chicago winter snow, had landed her on her butt in cold, not-quite-frozen mud. She still blamed Mr. Spencer Reed for putting her in the position of embarrassing herself with his insistence on interrupting her workday.

In contrast to her willed focus, her subconscious made clear her total lack of control, as thoughts of that man and his insulting offer continued to pop into her head throughout the day. During a meeting with one of her project managers, Addy caught herself comparing the brassy highlights of the man's strawberry-blond mop to the rich, gold glints she remembered in Spencer's hair. When she took a half hour to review a new proposal, the first residential property she'd been offered, she blinked herself out of a fantasy that the property Reed had mentioned might be a house as intriguing as the one she was being asked to work on. Even her lunch break was interrupted by constant thoughts of the witty, sarcastic comebacks she imagined herself using on the attorney in a world where her off-the-cuff remarks would outmatch his.

Stop it. Just stop it. She crumpled up the remains of her Italian sub sandwich in its wrapper and pitched it neatly into the wastebasket in the corner of her office. *I'm not interested in anything that man has to say.*

It was depressing, however, that Spencer was the first man in aeons to spark anything other than boredom in her. Not her type at all, but still…there was something about the arrogance, not to mention the body, the face and the very mussable hair, that made her want to get down on the floor and wrestle with him.

She shook her head once and commanded her sex drive to sit down and shut up.

And stop calling him Spencer, she berated herself. You don't call your enemies by their first names.

"Adeline Tyler, don't you dare tromp through my house in those mucky boots! Get back out on the porch."

Her mother's voice came rocketing out of the house before Addy had edged more than the toe of one boot over the threshold of the front door. By the time she bent down to begin unlacing her undeniably filthy boots, Susannah Tyler was planted firmly in the doorway, barricading the entrance until the offending articles were removed.

When the freezing air hit her toes, Addy realized that even her socks were soaked.

"Hi, Mom," she said, and stepped into the welcoming embrace, returning it with a fierceness that had her mother narrowing her eyes in concern.

"Hi, yourself." The concern switched gears as Susannah noticed the debris that had transferred to her own neatly pressed blouse and jeans. "Maybe I should take the rest of your clothes while we're at it."

"I'll take you up on that, but can I come inside first?" Addy asked, grinning, as she swung her mother gently around by the shoulders and stepped into the warmth of her childhood home. The boots, she left on the porch.

"Get in, get in." Her mother handed Addy a pair of slippers as she hustled her into the guest bathroom off the hall, disappearing and then returning moments later with a thick terry bathrobe. "Good Lord, girl. What happened to you?"

"Ladies' mud wrestling," she answered with a laugh, and stripped out of her clothes. Her mother accepted them gingerly with one hand. The bathrobe felt wonderfully clean. "It's my new career."

"And to think we could have saved all that money on your college tuition," her mother called as she headed back toward the kitchen. "There's coffee on, if you want some before you take a hot shower."

"Absolutely." She stepped into the sheepskin-lined slippers and followed her mother to the rear of the house. Through the smattering of architectural courses she'd taken for her own pleasure on her way to attaining a degree in civil engineering, she knew that her family's home was a perfect example of the Chicago bungalow, one of thousands clustered around the city. But in her heart, the house was unique. She'd spent two-thirds of her life in this house and now, as she did each time she came home, she walked slowly through the rooms, pausing in each one to savor the memories evoked by every square foot of space.

And the photographs. Nearly every table, most of the walls, any shelf with a spare inch of space on its ledge, held collections of the pictures that tracked the Tyler family in their continuing lives. Maxie in fabulously outrageous Halloween costumes. Tyler, two seconds before carrying out his threat to tackle the photographer. Herself, Sarah and her mother caught off guard in dozens of moments.

Most of all, though, what caught her were the pictures of her father. Michael McKinley Tyler had been killed in a car accident when Addy was eight years old. Maxie hadn't even been born yet. Addy knew she was the only one of his four children who could remember him clearly, remember his wickedly flashing dark eyes and the music he could pour out of his saxophone like a liquid-gold rain in their small living room. So she took special pleasure in the recognition that flowed warmly through her with every picture of his smiling face.

"Hi, Daddy." She blew a kiss at a photo of her father wailing away on the sax in the smoky darkness of a jazz club. Having greeted the house, she followed the dark aroma of French roast to the kitchen.

"Still the same as you remember?" her mother asked as she cracked the oven door and peered inside. Two mugs waited, steaming, on the butcher-block table.

Addy wrapped cold hands around the heavy ceramic mug and inhaled deeply, drawing in the rich scent. She'd first tasted coffee the day she turned six and the only thing she'd wanted for her birthday was to be allowed to watch her dad play with his band. Perched sleepily on a chair in the corner of the club, up far past her bedtime, waiting for the late set to start, her mother had let Addy sip a milky café au lait to stay awake. Smoke, jazz and coffee were inextricably linked for her from that night on.

"I think I'd run screaming out the door if you ever redecorated."

"Your brother and sisters would have me committed. But before they invade, how was your day? Other than finding your true career path in mud wrestling, that is."

"Disturbing." Her mother's raised eyebrow encouraged her to continue. Addy bit her lip and tried to find the right words for her questions. In the end, the simplest way seemed best. "Mom, did you know that Great-Aunt Adeline died?"

Susannah briefly closed her eyes and dropped her head beneath the light of the stained-glass lamp hanging above the table. When she looked back at Addy, her eyes, and her words, were calm. Measured. "Yes, I'd heard."

"Why didn't you tell us? Tell me?" If she hadn't known, Addy was sure her siblings were equally in the dark.

Her mother paused before speaking.

"You wouldn't even remember meeting her. You were just

a baby. But I used to send her pictures of you. Your brother and sisters, too, but I always hoped she'd feel some kind of bond with you at least. Since you were named for her." She shrugged. "I honestly didn't think you would even hear about it."

"Surprise, surprise," Addy murmured, mostly to herself.

"Who told you?"

"Aunt Adeline's attorney."

"What?" Confusion battled surprise on her mother's face.

"Apparently you were more successful than you thought. I've been named in her will." Addy's irritation blossomed anew at the mere thought. She knew her anger was a mixed-up tangle directed at both her great-aunt and Spencer Reed, but she resolutely shut thoughts of the disturbingly attractive man out of her head. "Maybe she thought she could buy her way back into your good graces on her deathbed."

Ceramic mug met wood tabletop with a forceful clatter.

"Watch your mouth, Adeline Marie Tyler." Her mother's voice crackled with real anger. "You may not live under my roof anymore, but in this house we don't disrespect the dead, or their last wishes."

Susannah jumped up and paced the tile floor, eventually stopping to yank plates and water glasses from a cabinet. She turned and thrust the stack of plates at her eldest daughter. "If Aunt Adeline changed her feelings at the end and then died before she found a way to tell us, that's the saddest thing I've ever heard. Go set the table."

Addy stood and took the dishes, but remained stubbornly in one spot.

"I don't want anything from her. She meant nothing to me."

Her mother cupped a hand against Addy's cheek, brushed a tangle of curls behind one ear. Gentleness rested in her touch.

The shrill peal of the telephone rang through the house.

"Answer that. Set the table. You'll figure the rest out later." Her mom patted her cheek and turned back to the stove.

She set the plates down in the dining room before heading to the tiny phone table in the hall. Answering the phone with her mind on other things, she was confused by the voice she heard. She moved the handset away from her ear, stared at it for a moment and then put it back.

"Excuse me? *Who* is this?"

"Spencer Reed, Ms. Tyler. I wanted to let you know—"

"How did you get this number? It's not even mine."

She could hear the impatience in his words and pictured his lips thinning as he pressed them together. "There are a lot of ways to get information if you're willing to pay for it. But in the case of your mother's home phone number, your aunt gave it to me years ago."

"Great-aunt," she shot back, not willing to let him claim an ounce more family intimacy than absolutely necessary. "It would have been kinder of her to use the number herself and call my mother just once in the last twenty or thirty years. Speaking of which, why doesn't this bequest go to my mother? She's the nearest relation. Or why not my brother and sisters, too? Why just me?"

He paused before speaking. She could picture him leaning back in an oversize leather chair, looking up at the ceiling. He would treat even her snippy questions with serious thought, she knew—and wondered why she was so certain of that.

"Maybe she thought it was too late to make amends to your mother but not too late to try with you. And you *are* her namesake. She felt that connection."

His voice had softened with the last words, but she refused to be drawn in on such a sentimental appeal. "How would you know? Are you in the habit of quizzing your clients about their intentions? Don't you just have to witness things and perhaps insult the client as a side benefit?"

Her shoulder was getting sore from leaning against the wall and she found herself twirling a curling strand of hair around one finger.

"Your great-aunt was more than just a client to me. Why don't you meet me for a drink or dessert after you and your family have finished dinner, and you can ask me all the suspicious questions you like?" He was teasing her, and she was glad he couldn't see her through the phone.

"Tell the truth. You're smiling just a little bit," he said.

She almost laughed.

What are you? Twelve? Why not just ask him to pass you a note during study hall? She stood up straight and shook her head, scowling at how easily she'd been suckered in, despite herself.

"I don't think—"

He cut her off immediately.

"Don't say anything. I'll be at Francesca's at nine. Do you know it?"

"I don't care how great their tiramisu is. I'm not waiting an hour for a table just to have coffee and dessert."

"No waiting. I know the owner."

"Of course you do." Everyone else in the city had to call a month in advance for a reservation and hope the maître d' was in a good mood. But he knew the owner. Of course. "Don't wait for me to order your coffee."

"Just think about it over dinner." She waited, already sure that he couldn't possibly hang up the phone without one last push at her. "Come and share something sweet with me, Addy Tyler. You might be surprised how much you like it."

She didn't know if he could hear her softly voiced, "Ha!" as she quietly depressed the off button on the phone, severing the connection. Let him wait. She had no intention of thinking about that man for one more minute of her evening.

The gust of freezing air that announced the arrival of one of her siblings drew goose bumps on Addy's skin beneath the terry robe. When the chill wind didn't stop, and the cacophony of sound accompanying it clarified into two feminine voices bickering at top volume, she sighed and headed to the front door.

"Close the door, creeps. There's snow enough outside without letting it in the house."

Her sisters turned as one at the sound of her voice. Maxie,

the baby, muttered one last dig at Sarah and sprinted over to Addy for a hug. Sarah, with raised eyebrows and a look of supreme frustration tensing her face, turned and shut the door.

Cold air radiated from Maxie's jacketed body as she squeezed her sister. Maxie stepped back and eyed Addy's attire, wrinkling her nose.

"Put on some pants. Vorks vonders vith ze chill factor," she said, her voice rolling with the heavy Russian accent of a wicked seductress from a James Bond flick.

"Dress yourself, brat." She paused to take in the enormous column of white fur perched precariously on Maxie's short, spiky curls. "Or maybe not. Nice hat, *Ivana.*"

"Today I am Russki, *nyet?*" Her voice lapsed back into its typical American youthful enthusiasm. "I couldn't resist, Addy. As soon as I saw it, all I could think about was horse-drawn sleighs and *daschas* in the woods and lots of ice-cold vodka in front of a roaring fire. Can't you just picture it?"

Even Sarah was smiling as she walked over to the two of them and slung an arm around each sister's shoulder for a group squeeze. Everyone in the family was used to Maxie's soaring flights of the imagination and her tendency to dress herself up to suit them. "Of course we can, Max," Sarah said. "And you can borrow my copy of *War and Peace* or *Anna Karenina* if you want to pick up a bit more atmosphere. Just please stop trying to set me up with that guy, okay? You may be acing art school, but postgrad veterinary science is kicking my butt. I just don't have time for a whirlwind romance right now. From what I've read, they seem to take up quite a lot of time and energy."

"Zat's vhy zey call zem *vhirlvinds,* dahlink." The playful accent was back, and forgiveness floated on the air kisses Maxie blew at Sarah. "And I'll take whichever book describes the clothes better, please."

"War and Peace," Sarah said decisively.

"I don't know how you read all of those incredibly *long* books, on top of all that studying," Addy whispered directly into her sister's ear as they turned and hugged each other hello. "Give me a nice, uncomplicated set of engineering plans any day."

Melting snowflakes sparkled like tiny jewels in Sarah's long, straight dark hair, the only one of the siblings not to inherit their parents' waves and curls. She poked a careful finger at Addy's still-muddy tangles. "It keeps me sane. And you liked *Jane Eyre*. Admit it."

"Yeah, sure. It was okay. But do you know how long it took me to read that thing?" Addy scoffed out loud, although she'd been wondering for the past month if she should ask her sister to recommend another book to her. Studying civil engineering hadn't afforded a lot of time to read grand, sweeping love stories, and she'd found herself oddly caught up in the story between the governess and the aristocrat, the tragedy and the joy of it.

"Let me guess. There was a fire at a farm and you had to stop, drop and roll in the pigsty, right?" Maxie's teasing words and gentle tug at her hair reminded Addy that she still needed to clean up for dinner.

"Trust me, and don't ask."

Family dinner at the Tyler family homestead was, as always, a raucous affair, as stories, complaints and triumphs came pouring out of all of them. Addy braced herself for the onslaught of opinion and advice as she dropped her bombshell.

Standing in front of the plate-glass living room window after dinner, her head was full of conflicting voices arguing caution versus a take-the-money-and-run approach. Watching the exhaust billow in clouds from her truck as it sat running on the street in her hopeful attempt to warm the interior before her drive home, she found herself pulling up a picture of the irritating Spencer Reed in her mind's eye. Dislike wound up with embarrassment, like a ball of snakes, settled heavily in her stomach as she recalled their childish bickering. She tried to remove her emotions from the equation, to look at her great-aunt's bequest fairly and without prejudice, and found that she couldn't do it.

No doubt Mr. Spencer Reed would have no difficulty shutting off his emotions and approaching the situation coldly and with a logical mind. But Addy couldn't stop herself from feeling angry and insulted.

She only hoped she wasn't letting her dislike of the urbane lawyer, with his pristine suits and polished manner, affect her good judgement.

"Take it, take it, take it, take it," the voice hissed softly in the quiet room.

After a brief moment of toe-curling startlement, Addy reassured herself that in fact neither the devil nor her subconscious was whispering to her in a disembodied voice from the coziness of her mother's living room.

"Speak to me, oh wise one," she intoned.

Her brother, several feet taller than the skinny brass lamp behind which he was attempting to hide, cocked his head to one side and grinned the grin that unraveled scores of women on a Friday night at Sully's Tavern as he walked over to her.

"I know this whole thing is freaking you out a little bit. I just think you should check it out is all. The woman is dead." He glanced over his shoulder toward the kitchen, as if expecting their mother to come running to scold. "No disrespect intended, but she can't hurt you now. Or make you do anything you don't want to do. So why not take the chance to go after something you've always wanted."

She knew her smile didn't quite reach her eyes as she hugged him, her handsome brother with the wicked smile and the dark eyes that reminded her so much of their father. He was the only one in her family who knew of her secret dream, probably because it echoed so strongly in him, too.

But she couldn't explain to him, because she didn't understand it herself, that somehow she *did* feel hurt. A small, sharp pain like a bruise had lodged itself in her chest ever since Spencer had told her that her great-aunt was dead.

"How did you get to be so wise at twenty-four?"

"Hey, everyone knows that bartenders are the world's

cheapest psychologists. Besides, I've always been smarter than you. Mom still thinks you're the one who broke her Belleek vase."

"Christopher Robin…" she warned. She was still ticked about that.

He winced. "Jeez, Addy, don't say that where people can hear you, will ya?"

Her brother's given name was a standing joke in the family. Claiming delirium from the pain of giving birth to a boy with such a big, fat head, their mother had years ago absolved herself of all responsibility. Outside the home, he introduced himself by his last name, and all the world knew him as Tyler.

Addy and her sisters were forbidden, on pain of severe sibling torture methods, to mention Christopher Robin Tyler's given name in public.

"It's written in the bylaws of sisterhood, baby brother," she teased. "Thou shalt torture thy brother at any opportunity." She stood up on tiptoe and pressed a kiss to his cheek. "I get busted out of the union if I let you slide."

His hands on her shoulders were gentle as he gave her a little shake.

"Just think about it," he said and walked her back over to the window to keep an eye on the running truck.

"I will," she promised.

After saying her goodbyes and collecting the copy of *Pride and Prejudice* Sarah had pulled off their mother's shelves with a smile at Addy's hesitant request, she stepped carefully down the slippery walk to her truck, heading for the short but chilly drive home.

When the snowball that exploded against the back of her head turned out not to contain rocks, she realized her baby brother really was grown up after all.

She had deliberately stayed late at her mother's house, but the temptation to drive by Francesca's and try to see in the plate-glass window front was nearly irresistible. At the intersection of the street that would let her perform a casual drive-by peek, she pulled over to the curb and sat through three changes of the light.

Had she been able to banish his voice from her head, she might have given in to the temptation to stop and see if he was still waiting for her.

But she couldn't get him out of her head. So she drove home.

Back in her one-bedroom apartment, she slid naked between the flannel sheets of her bed and pulled the down comforter up to her chin. By the light of a bedside lamp, she opened the covers of the book and tried to still all the noise in her head with the elegant words of another time and place.

She fell asleep in a confusing swirl of clipped British commentary on marriage, money and misunderstandings, with some smart-aleck Chicago commentary on the side. The opening sentence of Jane Austen's novel trotted on light feet in circles through her mind: "It is a truth universally acknowledged, that a single man in possession of a good fortune, must be in want of a wife."

In her last conscious thoughts before the dreams overwhelmed her, she wondered if, as a woman in possession of a good fortune, she'd have to watch out for rapacious wife hunters. And realized that she'd decided to find out more about Great-Aunt Adeline's bequest.

Racing out of her apartment building front door at five o'clock the next morning, already running late for a breakfast meeting, she came within inches of flattening the FedEx man.

After catching him and then listening to him crab about early morning deliveries, she signed where he pointed, her handwriting illegible with cold fingers in thick mittens, grabbed the package without examining it and ran for her truck.

Scraping the accumulated snow off her truck warmed her up a little, although the icy vinyl bench seat sucked the heat right back out of her bones when she slid her butt across it.

Hidden patches of black ice and a need to drive de-

fensively amidst skidding semi tractor-trailers necessitated a
strict eyes-on-the-road policy. Not until she made the slow
turn into her company's parking lot, rear wheels fishtailing a
little bit even at a crawl, did Addy have a safe moment to
glance at the return address on the FedEx envelope.

"Damn it!"

Shooting pain lanced up her leg as she rapped her knee
sharply against the dash, sliding out of the truck while glar-
ing at the blue-and-white envelope. She hobbled into the
building, smacked the offending object onto the middle of her
desk and limped off to dig up some much-needed coffee.

Voices echoing from the conference room reminded her
that their video teleconferencing call with the client from
Japan was about to begin.

She just needed one minute.

Ripping off the cardboard strip labeled Tear Here, she
yanked out the pages, and knew that if someone were to see
her and ask why she was snarling, she'd be unable to give a
good answer.

But just seeing that man's name on a return address made
her want to heave a rock through a plate-glass window.

Preferably his.

A handwritten note was paper-clipped to the top page.

A representative of the firm will be waiting at the following address this evening between 6:00 and 8:00 p.m.
if you would like to view the property mentioned in your
great-aunt's last will and testament. I hope you will not
allow any previous misunderstanding to scare you off.
Spencer Reed
P.S. The tiramisu was indeed excellent.

Fourteen hours later, Addy was still fuming.

Scare her off? *Scare her off?*

Her entire day had proved to be one disaster after another,
made worse by the fact that she couldn't keep her mind on

her work. Not that she was surprised. How could she concentrate when the strangulation fantasies were running through her head with such startling visual clarity?

Now, spotting an open parking space in the vicinity of the north-side address, she slewed her truck into the gap, grabbed her backpack, jumped out and marched up the block.

Fifty yards ahead of her, silhouetted by the glow of a streetlight, a tall figure leaned casually against a wrought-iron fence.

She didn't need the benefit of light to know who it was.

Two

Addy skidded to a halt on a patch of ice in front of the gate. He reached out a hand to steady her. She shrugged it off, glared up at his shadowed face and wished she were taller.

"What the hell are you doing here, Reed?"

"Good evening to you, too, Ms. Tyler."

"There's nothing good about it," she snapped, the words exploding in cloudy puffs of her breath in the icy air. "What are you doing here?"

His tone was carefully modulated to soothe. She felt as if she was being handled, and resented it.

"My note said—"

"Your note," she interrupted, "said a 'representative' of the firm would be here. Not *you*." A sharp poke at his shoulder emphasized her final word.

Addy had a split second to note that she might as well have poked a brick wall, for all he moved, before the recoil of her own rude gesture threw her off balance again, her low-heeled boots skating out from beneath her.

Spencer yanked her up against his body, one arm wrapped around her waist, the other hand cupping her elbow. The heat of him radiated through his tailored black coat, cashmere no doubt, and she blamed her momentary dizziness on the sudden warmth. She was aware that she should be backing away from him.

Neither of them moved.

Light reflecting softly off the snowdrifts lit a glimpse of summer sky in his eyes as his gaze slid over the contours of her face, coming to rest on her lips. She experienced it like a physical caress and felt her mouth soften in response. Dazed, she was already visualizing the kiss when his voice broke in with the hard crash of reality.

"I was afraid you wouldn't come."

"What?"

Blood rushed to her face as she jerked herself out of his arms, embarrassed to realize that she'd been mooning over the man like a lovesick teenager hoping for a kiss at the end of a first date.

She reached out a hand to the fence and steadied herself, feeling the twist of wrought iron radiate cold like an icy bone in her clenched fingers.

"I thought you might not come," he repeated patiently, tucking his hands carefully into his coat pockets. "Based on the outcome of our first meeting."

"Based on the—" She sucked in frigid winter air and welcomed the cold pain in her lungs as it swept the fog from her brain. "So you lied. And on top of that, you implied in your little note that I'd be too scared to show up."

"I thought that might get you here, even if it was only to yell at me. And since I am in fact a representative of the firm, I wasn't lying, strictly speaking."

"Tell me, Counselor, are the intimidation tactics part of your hourly billing, or did you charge my great-aunt extra for that?"

"I did what I had to do."

Back on firmer ground, squared off against him like a

prizefighter in the ring, she grabbed on to her anger and used it as a shield against other more confusing emotions. In the swirl of anger and attraction, of unwanted hurt and even more unwanted awareness of the man standing in front of her, the scents of old leather and warm vanilla spices still lingering on her clothes from where she'd been pressed up against him—*Jesus, the man even smelled rich*—one thing was clear. She should be asking herself the same question she'd thrown at him. What the hell was she doing here?

She didn't need this, any of it, and she didn't want it.

The realization settled like a burlap sack of wet sand on her shoulders, with none of the elevated light and joy she somehow thought she should feel upon deciding to walk away from her great-aunt, Spencer Reed and this entire mess.

"You did what you had to do." She repeated his words, rolling them slowly around in her mouth as if they were part of a new dish whose taste she wasn't sure she cared for. "Oh, that's right. I forgot. The rules of polite society don't apply to you, do they? You're a *lawyer.*"

She opened her mouth, the torrent of scathing words near to bursting the dam, when she realized that she was just prolonging the encounter. Her teeth clicked sharply together as she snapped her jaw shut, shook her head, turned and walked away.

"Addy, please."

The voice, low and quiet, calling her name the way a friend or a family member or a lover would, made her pause, though she didn't turn around. She'd known the man for less than two days and it already seemed like every time she tried to walk away from him, he managed to get one last word in.

"Just take a look at the place, please." The words slid around her like a gentle hand, curling around her elbow and tugging softly in his direction. "We'll both go inside and get warm, I'll explain some of the details to you and you won't take any potshots at my profession."

Her bark of laughter startled them both.

She had to see the look on his face after that, and the need brought her back to him where he stood in front of the wrought-iron gate up to his ankles in snow and looking perplexed by her sudden burst of laughter.

"You've *got* to be kidding." All at once, her humor in the situation was genuine. "*My* potshots at *your* profession?"

For once, Spencer's reserved facade slipped. She could see the physical moment when he remembered his comments to her the day before, and watched him visibly flinch. The sheepish grin and the brow slightly lifted in guilty acknowledgement begged her forgiveness, and the words swiftly followed.

"And I'll continue to apologize for my massive and completely unprofessional lack of courtesy yesterday morning. What do you say?"

Addy bit her lip, chewing off her raspberry-flavored Chap Stick and feeling the last bit of warmth seeping out of her body. She started to shiver. Lord, it was cold.

Spencer took a step toward her, bringing his face clearly into the light for the first time. The skin of his face as it followed the sharp contours of his cheekbones was pale. She wondered abruptly if he'd been standing outside this gate and waiting for her since six o'clock. She'd stubbornly delayed until the last minute before driving over here, a gesture that had felt independent at the time but now seemed merely childish.

"Addy." He stood close enough now to encompass her in his shadow, the streetlight behind him making a golden halo out of his hair. He lifted a hand and nudged her chin up with gloved fingers until her gaze met his again. She was conscious of her own breathing, the scratchiness of the knit wool cap pulled low on her brow, the dull ache in her fingers and toes. If she didn't pay attention, she might forget to take her next breath.

His thumb scraped lightly along her jaw. Tucked a rampant curl behind her ear. Her ears were ice.

"Addy, it's not really me that you're mad at here."

Like the ice of a frozen lake cracking beneath the blades

of a skater, the moment shattered. Irritated again, she snapped a wave at the gate.

"Let's get on with it, Reed. And keep the psychoanalysis to yourself. If I want a therapist, I'll hire one who doesn't know how to sue me sixteen ways from Sunday." She raised her hands in the air, cutting off any response. "Sorry."

"Right." He exhaled sharply. A set of keys jangled in his hand as he wrestled with the frozen lock on the gate. "Sorry about the hedges. Your great-aunt meant to have them cut back, but time got away from her."

For the first time, Addy noticed the towering wall of hedges pressing against the fence, leaning heavily over the iron spikes capping the fence rails. Branches struggled to squeeze through the narrow gaps between rails, reaching out to snag unwary pedestrians. Icicles as thick as her wrists pulled heavy boughs earthward in dangerous arcs.

"Jesus," she breathed. "It's the briar wood surrounding Sleeping Beauty's castle."

When Spencer laughed, she simply raised an eyebrow at him. "You know, all those knights in shining armor impaled themselves on the thorns and died horribly painful deaths in those hedges."

"Well, then, I guess it's a good thing I left my armor at home today," he said, swinging the gate wide open before her. "Come on in, Sleeping Beauty."

"Right," she muttered as she stepped onto a clean-swept walk that drew a straight line to the front door. Or presumably it did. At the moment, with the snow-laden heights of the hedges blocking off the street, the yellow wedge of light arcing in from the gate was the only illumination. Although she could pick out the outline of the house—high, peaked roofs and other mysterious shapes—against the light of the city sky, details of the building itself were invisible.

"Got a flashlight, Reed?"

"Dammit. If the power's out again…" Spencer brushed past her. "Stay here. I'll be right back."

"Again?"

She stomped her feet and crossed her arms tightly against her chest. After a minute or two, a light flickered from what looked like a porch. The man had apparently dug up his own flashlight.

"I'm going to check the fuse box…" His voice echoed slightly, as if reaching out to her from far off instead of across the lawn. "…be just one more minute."

Three minutes later, after a particularly stiff gust of wind dumped a load of snow off a branch two feet in front of her head, Addy gave up on waiting. She'd damn well rather stand in a dark hallway than out here in the Arctic Circle. Picking her feet up high with finicky cat steps through the newly dumped snow, she approached the darkened house.

When the lights snapped on, she threw a hand in front of her face, reflexively blocking the sudden glare.

And then lowered her hand one millimeter at a time, her mouth hanging open and her eyes painfully wide.

It was a castle.

Towers and turrets. Candles flickering in sheltered sconces. The hedges, threateningly visible in the sudden light, loomed over her like the encroaching boundaries of an ancient forest. She could almost swear she heard horns, dying faintly away on the cold night air, calling the hounds to hunt.

When the wolf burst around the side of the building and raced straight toward her, giving one deep *woof* on the way, Addy decided that she was hallucinating. Clearly.

Her next conscious thought was that being body-slammed by a wolf into a snowbank sure did shoot the hallucination theory all to hell. Its paws were planted smack in the middle of her stomach and she could feel its hot breath on her neck as it shoved its nose beneath her scarf. She opened her mouth to scream.

And sputtered in disgust as she got a faceful of doggy drool when the thing licked her from her chin to her eyebrows.

"Ew, gross, disgusting." She whipped her head to the side

to avoid another lick and spat into the snow. "Get *off* me, you big lug."

"Elwood! Heel!"

The dog gave a reluctant whine, swiped one last kiss wetly across her forehead and leapt off her to go trotting obediently away. Addy pushed herself up on her elbows, scraped the snow out of her collar and wished that the heat of her irritation could actually shoot red laser beams out of her eyes to burn to a crisp the man striding across the snow-covered lawn toward her.

"I'm so sorry. I didn't realize he was out." Spencer came to a halt at her feet. She could see him trying to decide whether or not it would be safe to offer her a hand up. The dog, an enormously overgrown puppy she now saw, bounced around his feet, tail wagging and tongue drooling. "Elwood, sit. Sit, Elwood."

When Spencer finally gave up and shoved the dog's butt into the snow with two gloved hands, Addy laughed out loud.

"Elwood?" she asked as she clambered to her feet and started brushing off her clothes. "Let me guess, he has four whole fried chickens for lunch every day."

"That was Jake. Elwood ate dry white toast."

"That giant wolf in dog's clothing certainly eats more than white toast." She could feel melting snow trickling down the back of her neck. "What kind of dog is it anyway?"

"Elwood's a purebred Akita."

"Of course. Even her dog sounds snotty, though I wouldn't have thought Great-Aunt Adeline was a fan of *The Blues Brothers.*"

"I don't think she ever saw the film. Elwood is my dog."

Oops. So much for the truce on insults.

Before she could ask what his dog was doing at the house, Addy heard Spencer give what sounded suspiciously like a snicker. She glared up at him. His lips were clamped together in what was clearly a weak effort to keep from laughing out loud at her. "If you're finding this funny, Reed…" she warned.

"Not at all," he said, his voice strangled. "It's just…dripping." He reached out a gloved hand toward her hair.

"Don't touch me," she snapped, and jerked her head back. This had the unfortunate effect of dislodging the mountain of snow perched on her hat, spilling it down her face in a cold, damp mini avalanche.

"Dammit."

Spencer's laughter burst out of him in an uncontrollable guffaw. Through the ice water dripping into her eyes, she saw him strip off his gloves and shove them into the pockets of his overcoat. He stepped through the snow to stand next to her, crowding her.

"You're invading my personal space, Reed. Back off." She knew she looked ridiculous, and resented it.

"I'm cleaning you up, Frosty. Relax." He tugged off her knit cap and ran his bare fingers gently through her wet curls, combing out clumps of melting snow. She felt the trails left by his fingers on her scalp like the burning afterimage of the sun. Spencer brushed his thumbs gently across her eyebrows and then her cheekbones. When his fingers passed softly over her mouth, she inhaled shakily, and the sudden narrowing of his eyes told her that he'd heard it. "And it wouldn't kill you to call me by my first name, Addy."

"You know, it just might," she muttered, and nearly smiled at the grimness in her own voice. Her awareness of his hands on her skin shocked her with its intensity. In a sudden movement, she jerked her hands up to push his away, only to find her fingers entangled with his.

If I'm so cold, why does it feel like he's burning me? As the words flashed through her brain, she tried to pull her hands away.

"That's enough."

"Not nearly."

The clouds of their breaths lingered in the cold, still air between their faces, merging into one slowly disappearing fog. Addy felt the ridiculous urge to tuck her top lip over her bottom one and direct her next breath straight at her feet, and told herself she was being paranoid.

She didn't think she sounded very convincing.

"Your hands are cold."

Her fingers were still interlocked with his, and Spencer was rubbing them gently. With inexorable slowness, he pulled her hands to his mouth and exhaled warmly on them. When she shivered, his smile showed in his eyes.

Enough was enough.

"I'm soaking wet because of your goofy dog, Reed. I'm cold all over," she snapped.

For the second time since her arrival, her irritation at his smugness saved her from further embarrassment. She yanked her hands away from his and shoved them deep into her coat pockets. "I suppose it would be too much to ask to go inside now, before I end up with a raging case of pneumonia?"

Spencer's grin told her she wasn't fooling anyone. Then she shivered again, and this time it was because she actually was freezing.

"I really am cold," she said as her teeth started to chatter.

"Of course. Come on." With a casualness she didn't fall for, he snagged one of her hands and tucked it in the crook of his arm. He led the way back to the sidewalk and steered her toward the front porch. After a moment of mental debate, Addy decided that the advantage of not having to look where she was going, allowing her to stare at the house looming over them, was worth the inconvenience of bumping into Spencer's body with every step. Elwood pranced about their feet, kicking up snow with a dog's sheer joy in play.

But it was the house, the fairy-tale, castlelike vision of a house, that she couldn't take her eyes off.

With all of the lights on and a little more composure under her belt, Addy could see that although the house was large, it was the height of the building that made it seem so imposing. The house itself was three full stories tall, and its towers—*there are towers, with round walls and cone-capped roofs, for God's sake*—stretched another story or two higher. There were windows everywhere, almost more windows than walls it seemed, and warm yellow light shone out of dozens of them.

Closer to the house, she started to realize why the building gave off such a feeling of age. Her initial impression of stone walls had been given by the mottled, peeling gray paint on the clapboard siding. The wraparound porch that stretched across the front of the house and around one side lent an air of elegant welcome, until she noticed that the gutters were pulling away from the porch roof in several places.

"Careful here. Watch your step."

"I see Great-Aunt Adeline didn't exactly keep the place up," she said as she gave a little leap over the first stair, most of which seemed to be missing, up to the porch.

"She was ninety-two when she died, Addy. New paint didn't exactly top her list of priorities." Spencer kept his gaze directly ahead of him, but his clipped enunciation communicated his displeasure well enough.

"I'm a little tense."

She knew her words weren't an apology, could hear her mother's voice in her head demanding that she make one, but Addy felt as if she'd done enough apologizing to this man already.

"I know." Spencer's hand tightened around hers for a moment and he turned his head to look directly at her. His eyes were the blue of the sky a half hour after sunset. Then he let go and reached for the door.

"I know." She mouthed the words at his back like a bratty five-year-old. Of course he does. Spencer Reed knows everything.

It was amazing how easily this man could get under her skin with just two words.

"Come inside. I'll find you some dry clothes." He called the words back over his shoulder at her as he pushed open the front door and then stepped quickly up the staircase directly in front of the door.

"I'm not going to be here long enough—" she started to call out after his retreating back "—to change clothes." She ended by talking to herself. "Sheesh. Like talking to a brick wall."

Might as well check the place out, Addy thought. Then she actually looked around her and realized that she would have no idea where to start. A long hallway extended on either side of the staircase toward the rear of the house, and what seemed like a dozen doorways opened off it, scattered randomly on both sides of the hall. Even the doorways themselves were varied, some with doors, some without. One was arched and another was an open cutout in the shape of the minaret of a Turkish mosque.

Flipping a mental coin, she started walking slowly down the right side of the hall, trailing her fingers along a chair rail. A faded Oriental runner muffled the sounds of her boots on the hardwood floors.

Above the chair rail, the walls were crowded. Oil paintings, photograph collages, dried flowers, even an old violin, were displayed with care for visual pleasure all the way down the hall. Addy stopped in front of an age-darkened portrait of a dark-haired woman with her hair pulled back severely in a bun and a small smile on her lips. The family resemblance was unmistakable, even if Addy couldn't have guessed the century for the life of her. Surprised, she found herself wondering if this was where her mother's habit of blanketing her walls with photographs and artwork and family mementos came from.

Reaching out a hand, she traced the line of the woman's cheekbone, her fingertips a millimeter from the painting's surface. An angular scribble in the corner of the painting caught her eye. After a moment's examination, she realized that the scribble was numbers.

1899.

Spiderlike chills crawled over her skin, lifting the hairs on her arm. This picture of a woman who looked so much like her mother, her sisters, herself, was over one hundred years old. Some quick math allowed her to guess that she was staring at a picture of her own great-great-grandmother.

"Her name was Susannah."

She jumped and clenched her jaw to keep from yelping at the sudden noise. One hand pressed firmly to her chest, she took a deep breath.

"Don't *do* that," she said. "You could kill someone." Spencer was holding out a pile of neatly folded clothes. She ignored it. A grin quirked across his face.

"Sorry." His voice didn't sound very apologetic. He looked at the portrait. "I don't even know who she is, but Adeline used to stop and look at that painting all the time. She told me once that the woman's name was Susannah."

"Susannah is my mother's name," she said after a long silence. "I think she was my great-great-grandmother." Something was cracking inside her. What felt like an enormous pressure burst into existence behind her eyes and in her temples. She took a breath and felt it hitch alarmingly in her chest. Shook her head and closed, then opened, her eyes. "Is there a bathroom here?"

"Second door down. Take these with you." Spencer pushed the clothes into her hands and she grabbed at them reflexively.

In the bathroom, she dropped the clothes on a green marble counter, cranked on the hot water and thrust her hands under the strong rush out of the antique taps. Everything was cold. Her hands felt like clattering ice cubes. She looked up and into a mirror and saw that her teeth were chattering.

No wonder I'm out of it—I really am about to come down with pneumonia. Time to stop being stupid just to prove I'm stubborn.

Five minutes later, she felt almost human again. Her jeans were still damp and chilly—taking her pants off was more comfortable than she'd wanted to get. But wearing a faded navy sweatshirt with Duke University emblazoned across the chest and thick, dry socks returned a little of her calm.

Duke?

She followed the sound of a whistling kettle and found Spencer in a tiny servant's kitchen, not much more than a closet with a hot plate and a sink, off the other hall. He'd removed his overcoat, suit jacket and tie somewhere along the way and stood in gray slacks and a deep blue button-down with the sleeves rolled up. She stood in the doorway, reluctant to squeeze into the tiny room with this man who made all the little hairs on her arms stand on end.

"So, Great-Aunt Adeline was a big Blue Devils fan, was she?"

When he looked startled at her sudden appearance, she was pleased. Let him be the one off balance for a little while. His gaze skimmed over her from head to toe. She saw his eyes narrow and guessed that he'd noticed she still wore her wet jeans.

"Not that I'm aware of. That's mine," he answered as he returned to pouring tea from a fat ivory pot into two bone-china teacups. "Did the sweatpants not fit?"

"I don't know," she said, watching him pour. She found it irritating that instead of looking silly or a bit prissy with a teapot, the contrast between the fragility of the china and the muscles in Spencer's hands and forearms only emphasized the strength of his physical presence in the tiny room. "I have this thing about wandering around big, empty houses with guys I don't know while wearing their pants. I'd rather keep my own, thanks. So tell me, why are your dog and your sweatpants at my great-aunt's house?"

His next words confirmed her suspicions.

"I've been staying here for a while," he answered, dropping what she could only assume was an actual tea cozy over the pot and then turning to her. "Do you take anything in your tea?"

"I have no idea. I never drink it. Is living in my great-aunt's house one of the perks of attorney-client privilege?"

"Of course not. Don't you read anything?" He doctored both teacups with a dollop of honey and a splash of milk and placed them on saucers. "Let's sit in the library. I'll start a fire.

You can warm up and I'll tell you about all the information *inside* that useful packet of papers I sent you this morning."

Trailing him down the hall, Addy felt like a fifth grader caught throwing spitballs during the teacher's pop quiz. She had deliberately ignored the stack of legal documents since she had no intention of accepting the bequest. Now she realized that when dealing with Spencer Reed, it was better at all times to be fully prepared. She was clumsy enough around him without choosing to be ignorant, also.

The library was a long, narrow room that turned out to contain not only books and a fireplace but also a half-dozen glass-fronted cases holding collections of everything from iridescent pinned butterflies to small, fossilized sea creatures to dusty hunks of various minerals and semiprecious crystals. It was as if walking into a turn-of-the-century curio museum, and Addy tumbled straight into love at her first sight of its jumbled oddities.

"Here, curl up and get warm." Spencer handed her tea to her and waved at a leather armchair with a muted plaid blanket draped over the arm.

She was more than happy to follow that order, and wrapped herself in the soft chenille throw while he squatted down in front of the fireplace and began fiddling with the stacked logs. His preoccupation allowed her to indulge in a lengthier look at the room around her. She was debating whether or not she ought to get up out of her comfy seat to take a closer look at some of the volumes on the far wall when she realized that her gaze, for the last several minutes, had been focused on the way the fabric of Spencer's clothes stretched tightly against his shoulders and his butt as he leaned forward with the long fireplace match and lit the kindling.

Give yourself a break, girl, she thought, and raised the teacup to her lips to hide her smile. There's no harm in looking, is there?

Just how much harm there could be was made clear, however, when Spencer suddenly turned and walked away from the fire, catching her stare. His grin rose like a slow tide on his face and she flushed. She would have sworn the dratted man could actually read her mind.

"Not too warm?" he asked, settling himself in the chair next to hers, tea in hand.

"Not at all," she said, denying the heated redness of her cheeks.

"Good, then we can get started." With these words, he leaned forward, bracing his forearms on his knees. "First of all, did you read *any* of the papers I sent you?"

"You mean the papers that arrived at five this morning?" she retorted smartly. The blatant lie was her best option. "I was in nonstop meetings all day long. I didn't have the time."

"I'm sure." His drawl bordered on insulting and the way he sat meant his clasped hands rested only inches from her knees. She tucked her legs up beneath her in the chair. "What is it that you do? No poor-taste joke to follow," he added.

"I'm a civil engineer." Gotcha, buddy, she thought, as her words made him sit up a little and cock his head a little to the side. And you can just ask me what that means if you don't know.

The silence held.

That was unexpected, Spencer thought. A civil engineer. He leaned back again in his seat and picked up his cup of tea, using the gesture to fill time as he thought about the implications. If she'd said she was an animal trainer for the circus, or a performance artist who did weird things onstage while reciting poetry under a black light, he wouldn't have been surprised. Adeline had told him stories about her niece, Addy's mother, who'd gotten pregnant and run off with a jazz musician at eighteen years old. So he was prepared for a little oddity in the mother's daughter. And she certainly had a mouth on her that defied polite-society conversation.

A civil engineer. Although he wouldn't want to be put on the spot to define what exactly that was—something to do with how a building affected the land and hooked up to various public-works systems, he thought—he was sure that you didn't get to be one by having a few screws loose. She'd likely done postgraduate work in a scientific field and held licenses from several federal and state boards.

This changed things. He wasn't sure how, but he *was* sure that it did.

First, a guess.

"Were you in the field yesterday morning?"

"How perceptive of you."

Tromping around on a construction site went a long way toward explaining her mud-bespattered appearance at his office. Still, even now she looked more like an unemployed college student, with her wildly curly black hair and what he felt sure were braless curves under his sweatshirt. She had silver rings—some braided, some set with stones, some plain—on almost every finger of both hands, including her thumbs.

But, an engineer.

"Please don't be offended if I tell you that that was not what I expected." He decided that honesty would be best, and waited to see if she would spring out of her chair and attack him for it.

"You mean like I didn't expect to find you living in my great-aunt's house?" she asked with a real smile. She was warm. She was cozy. There wasn't enough energy left in her body right now to get into a fight. Elwood strolled in the library door and flopped down in front of the fire. That's how she felt, too.

"Yes, something like that." He smiled at her, crinkling the corners of his ocean-blue eyes, and for the first time, she just smiled right back at him. The firelight was doing interesting things to his hair, dancing bronze and gold sparks off the ends. As their gazes held, she felt those same sparks take up dancing in her stomach.

"You're going to explain that, right?" she asked at last, cutting through the building tension with her voice.

He laughed. "Don't worry. It's only temporary while my condo is being renovated. I knew Adeline my whole life. My family have been her family's lawyers for almost a century, and when she heard I was going to move into a hotel, she invited me to stay here."

"Really?"

"Cross my heart. You can ask my mother." The thought of meeting the society matron who'd raised him did not excite her. "I hate hotels."

"Me, too," she murmured and curled up a little more in her blanket. The warmth of the fire was so soothing on her face, the low crackling of the flames hypnotizing. "So tell me what's in all those papers."

"Certainly. You should know, first of all, that this last version of your great-aunt's will was drawn up just last year. Since there are no other living relatives outside of your family, there should be no contesters as to the validity of the will. Assuming you fulfill the conditions of the bequest, there will be no…"

Spencer's measured baritone was very calming. His tone of voice asserted that there were no problems in this world that reflection and clear thinking could not solve. She was so reassured, in fact, that she thought she'd just rest her eyes for a moment while he spoke. She could listen to his very reasonable description of the terms of the will while she relaxed just a little bit after what had been an extremely long, tense day.

She fell asleep as she was listening to the conditions of the bequest, her sleepy brain certain that everything seemed very reasonable indeed. She even nodded her approval.

The room was silent when she next had a conscious thought. She wondered why the fire wasn't snapping and hissing. She considered opening her eyes to look at it.

Too much effort.

Someone was stroking her hair, she realized fuzzily. Static electricity had strands pulling away from the side of her face as the hand drew away. Gentle fingers returned to tuck the hair behind her ear.

Her eyes drifted open slowly. Spencer was crouched down

at her side, one arm draped along the chair back, fingers tangled in her hair. His other hand rested on her knee. She felt a physical *click* run through her system as his gaze locked with hers, bringing her closer to wakefulness.

"You know, you're incredibly beautiful when you sleep." His voice was soft and low. Maybe she was still asleep. Now he was smiling at her. "It helps that your mouth is shut."

His shadow fell over her first as he leaned toward her and then captured her lower lip between his and sucked on it lightly. She opened her mouth in surprise and he immediately covered it with his own, his tongue smoothly curling around hers in a dizzying attack on her senses. She was electrically conscious of where his hand was tracing small circles on her knee.

"What—" Her voice was sleep-rough as she tried to speak between kisses.

"You're beautiful," he murmured. She could feel the vibrations of his voice against her lips. "When you sleep." His mouth pressed hers open again.

Someone was moaning softly. Addy was afraid it was her. As her body surged into awareness of this man who was kissing her, who she wasn't even sure she liked but whose touch was turning her insides into a puddle of melted wax, her brain struggled to recall how she'd gotten into this situation.

His teeth nipped at her lower lip. He swallowed her sudden gasp. Her fingers were running themselves of their own will around his neck and dipping, touching him beneath the collar of his shirt.

She couldn't think. Tried harder. His hand was skating up the outside of her jean-clad thigh. He had been talking, explaining something about the will. Fingers slid under the bottom of her borrowed sweatshirt and skimmed the bare skin at her waist. There was the house and the money. His hand kneaded firmly at her hip. Something about living here for six months. His mouth was fiercer on hers now, the pressure arcing her head back and pressing her breasts into his chest. There was more, though, she was sure of it.

She had it.

With a near shriek of rage, she tore her mouth from Spencer's and shoved hard at his shoulders. Scrambled to get her numbed legs out from under her and clawed her way past him and out of the chair. Standing in the evening-dark room in her stocking feet in front of the embers of a banked fire, a blanket half draped over her shoulders, she only wanted the answer to one question.

Could she possibly have heard him correctly?

"Did you say that I have to be married?"

Three

"Ow."

Spencer looked up from his plate and across the corner of the long dining room table.

"Just pinching myself," Addy said, sucking at the sore spot on the back of her hand. The silver fork and knife in her hands were heavy, another world from her stainless-steel utensils at home. "Thought I must have been dreaming to agree to stay here tonight."

He tore his eyes away from the sight of her lips pulsing against her own skin. "Look outside. It's like the blizzard of '76 all over again." He pointed to the velvet-draped windows. She didn't turn to look at the swirling clouds of white made only more opaque by the light shining out of the room into the night. "You can't drive in that, even if we could manage to dig out your truck."

She glared at him. They'd already gone a few rounds about the fact that he'd let her sleep for three hours in front of the fire. He'd found it difficult to defend his decision since he

wasn't at all sure why he'd done such a thing. Being attracted to this prickly, sarcastic, hotheaded witch was one thing,
but making sure she'd be stranded for the night with him was
such a ridiculous strategy that he was startled to have given
in to it.

He'd watched her struggle to pay attention to his words as
the first wavelets of sleep began washing over her, then seen
her head nod in approval of what he was saying even as he
knew she was miles away in dreamland. And at first, he'd just
meant to let her nap for a few minutes.

He had watched her sleep. Ruddy shadows and warm gold
highlights had flickered over her face in the dancing light of
the fire. Without her usual anger and defensiveness animating
it, her face had looked like that of a teenager, the curves
of her lips parted just enough for breath. Violet watercolor
smudges had tinted the delicate skin around her eyes. She'd
tucked her hands beneath her cheek, and the small, birdlike
bones of her wrists had highlighted her aura of fragility.

He nearly snorted out loud, catching himself in the middle of this ridiculous reverie. Addy Tyler was about as fragile as a lead pipe, and she bent as much as one, too. It had been
a battle every step of the way to get her to set foot in this
house. He didn't know why it mattered so much to him that
she understand what she was giving up with her obstinate re-
fusal to have anything to do with her great-aunt's estate. He
only knew that he'd planned to drag her to the house screaming for the police all the way if necessary.

The last thing he'd expected was to see this stubborn, un-
sympathetic woman brought to the edge of tears by an old
family portrait, an emotion that he knew surprised her as
much as it did him.

He was beginning to wonder if that momentary glimpse of
softness would turn out to be his downfall.

Of course, since at the moment she was only speaking to
him when absolutely necessary, there didn't look to be much
chance of the two of them falling anywhere together.

On the upside, at least she wasn't yelling at him anymore. It was almost peaceful right now, sitting at the same table and sharing a meal.

"This is very—" he began.

Silverware clattered as Addy threw her knife and fork onto her plate and shoved her unfinished meal away, an expression of disgust twisting her face.

Perhaps he'd spoken too soon.

"Was she insane?" she demanded. "I have a right to know whether there's a history of mental derangement in my family. It might affect my decision to have children someday." She threw herself back in her chair and crossed her arms on her chest. "Don't give me that look. I'm being about as rational as good old Great-Aunt Adeline was in her will."

He didn't think this was the right time to mention that Adeline had considered Susannah's branch of the family tree to be the unstable one. He'd settle for a smaller measure of the truth. "Your great-aunt was in her right mind until the day she died."

"Says you," she said, knowing she was displaying the maturity level of a two-year-old. She blamed her crankiness on leftover sexual tension. Waking up to what had at first seemed a continuation of a sensual daydream, she'd been overwhelmed by the slow pulse of sensation throughout her body. Her memory of Spencer's description of the will's terms, and her anger, were life preservers she'd clung to with the desperate grasp of a person swept overboard.

She was hanging on still.

"She was nuts."

"Maybe she was just trying to make sure that you were, um…" Spencer paused for a moment. Was he hesitating? "That you were taken care of."

Of all the insulting… "I don't need a husband to take care of me." She tried to keep her tone below that of a shout as she jerked out of her chair and stood next to the table. She didn't think she'd been successful. "I take care of myself just fine, thank you. Where's the kitchen?"

"All the way at the back of the house."

She collected her tableware and squelched the thought that she was being rude beyond belief, leaving her host sitting at the table, finishing the meal that he had made for the two of them. Hey, at least she was clearing her own dishes.

At the end of the long hall, she found the kitchen, an enormous cavern of a room that ran most of the width of the back of the house. The faint odors—tomato and spicy sausage—of the Italian dinner Spencer had put together while she'd slept still lingered in the air. The room seemed to have been built before the advent of dishwashers, so she dumped her plate in the sink, determined to turn her back on the washing up and use some of her involuntary jail time here to explore the house.

She got as far as the door to the hall.

"A slave to my upbringing," she muttered two minutes later, up to her elbows in soapsuds and dirty dishes. The freedom to wander the house wasn't worth listening to her mother's voice in the back of her head, haranguing her for leaving the cook to do the cleaning. She'd tossed the pots and pans from the stove into the sink for good measure. No sense doing a half-assed job.

The house was old enough to give her fair warning when Spencer followed her into the kitchen minutes later, floorboards creaking from under the rug in the hall. His footsteps in the kitchen were silent. They'd both ditched their wet, snow-caked shoes soon after entering the house.

But she didn't need to hear him to know when he stood behind her, too close. She could see his reflection in the window above the sink, but more, she felt the warmth of him radiating into her. Imagined his breath stirring her hair. Pictured it until she could *feel* the strands stirring and then had a hard time keeping her wet hands from grabbing the back of her neck to still the shivers she felt there.

"Did you want something, Reed?" She rapped the question out like a drill sergeant, trying to shatter her awareness of him standing behind her, breathing.

His arm sneaked into the corner of her vision as he reached

past her to put his plate on the counter to the side of the sink. As she opened her mouth to snarl at him again, she felt a light weight drop onto her shoulder. A dish towel. At the same moment, Spencer snaked his hands down the length of her arms until his fingers tangled with hers in the hot water. He tugged her hands up.

"I'll finish up here." His voice was normal, denying the intimacy of their position. She was caged between his arms, between the solid strength of his body pressed against her back and the edge of the counter against her hips. She shivered and knew he felt it.

"Don't be ridiculous. Those who cook don't clean."

"Addy." He let go, dragged the towel off her shoulder and wrapped it around her hands, then turned her to face him. He ducked down a little to capture her downturned eyes with his own. She stopped avoiding them. "I'm sorry you're stuck here for the night. But since you are, you're my guest, and guests don't scrub pots."

He smiled at her and her stomach tripped and fell down an elevator shaft. Did his eyes have to be so damn blue?

"Besides—" he gave her a little push toward the door to the hall "—I know you're dying to take a look around."

She stuttered to a halt and turned back to him, hands still cocooned in the towel. "I like it better when you're not being so nice to me."

He covered the smile well. "I know."

She threw the towel at his head.

Catching the cloth one-handed, he turned to the sink with sublime indifference to her scowl. He waggled fingers in the air over his shoulder.

"Run along. I'll find you when I'm done here."

She stuck her tongue out at his back.

"That's very mature."

Damn. She'd forgotten that he could see her in the window's reflection. Time to get out before she made even more of an ass out of herself.

She ignored the central staircase for the time being, its two sets of stairs crossing like department-store escalators in the middle, one coming from the front and one from the back of the house. There were still more rooms on the ground floor that she'd yet to venture into.

The house faced west and was split in half by the massive staircase, with rooms opening to the north and the south off the side halls that ran the length of the building. The library butted up against the kitchen, at the rear of the north side of the house, with the tiny tea closet behind the next door as she walked slowly toward the front of the house. Another bathroom came next, this one done in shades of cream and palest gold.

The last room, at the very front of the house, was long enough that two sets of intricately carved wooden doors that slid into recesses in the walls opened onto it from the hall. She entered at the near set.

She felt as if she'd stepped into a Jane Austen novel.

It was a music room. Or at least that was what she supposed you would call it. Mossy green walls imposed an atmosphere of meditative calm, with framed copies of what looked like original music scores scattered here and there. At the front of the room, where light from the windows would fall upon it as the sun set, was a massive ebony grand piano. A harp, gilded and taller than she was, stood in the middle of the room near a clustered arrangement of chairs and sofas. Balancing the room at the near end was another piano, this one smaller and oddly constructed.

A small, framed black-and-white photograph just inside the door caught her eye. The image was of a young woman in a long, dark skirt and a pale blouse, cradling a violin in her arms. She wondered if the violin was the same as the one she'd seen in the hall earlier.

Then she wondered if the woman in the photograph was her great-aunt.

"My grandfather saw her play once." Spencer spoke from

the doorway. Not startled because she'd somehow known the moment he entered the room, Addy stared at the photo.

"Great-Aunt Adeline?" It felt embarrassing to admit that she didn't recognize her. She tried willing some sort of recognition beyond that of similar bone structure. If this woman *was* a part of her family, shouldn't she feel more of a connection with her image?

"Yes, with the CSO. The Chicago Symphony Orchestra." At least Spencer didn't seem to think it too odd, her not knowing what her own great-aunt looked like.

"I'm not an idiot, you know. I know what the CSO is." Though, truth be told, she would probably have had to think about it for a bit. Highbrow culture wasn't exactly her thing.

"He said she was absolutely luminous. That he couldn't take his eyes off her, onstage."

"So why did she quit playing?" She turned away from the photo and leaned against the wall, watching him. He'd unrolled his sleeves but had not rebuttoned the cuffs.

Spencer shrugged. "I don't know. Grandfather said that years later, he and his wife would invite her to join them in their box at the symphony and that she always turned them down. Every time. As far as he knew, after she stopped playing, she never attended another performance in her life."

"Strange."

"Sad."

They stood in companionable silence for a bit. For no good reason, Addy found herself sighing a little, so she straightened and looked around the room again. Spencer blinked and seemed to shake off an invisible net of distraction. They walked together to the piano.

"Do you play?" she asked, tilting her head to look at him. She could see the curve of his cheek rise as he smiled.

"Ten years of lessons as a kid," he said and laughed. "You would think that I could."

"Twins, separated at birth," she intoned with an emcee's exaggerated voice. She ran her palm along the sleek wood of the propped piano lid. Catching his confused look, she continued, "I don't think I made it through ten years, but it was a lot. And all I can play today is the first page of the theme to *The Pink Panther.*"

"Isn't that just the same four chords over and over again? Da-dunh, da-dah. Da-dunh, da-dah. And so on?" he teased from the opposite side of the baby grand.

"Hey, put up or shut up," she said, laughing. "What can you play?"

"Aside from 'Chopsticks'?" He slid onto the piano bench, stared at the keyboard for a moment and then started playing a ragtime melody with one hand, fumbling occasionally for a note. Thirty seconds later, he stopped and she applauded the effort with enthusiasm. He scooted off the end of the bench near her, took a quick bow and grinned. "'The Entertainer,' Scott Joplin. First page, right hand only."

"Congratulations. You've got me beat." She waved a hand at the rest of the room. "Got any other masterpieces in you?"

He shook his head. "Are you kidding? The harp is for girls—mind you, this is how I thought at ten years old—and only old people listen to the harpsichord." She guessed that was the odd-looking piano at the other end, glad she hadn't embarrassed herself by not knowing what it was. "The piano wasn't the trumpet or the sax, but it was still vaguely cool."

"My dad was a sax player," she said. She felt the words settle like a blanket over the room, muffling the brief burst of good humor between the two of them. She regretted it, but couldn't resist the urge to talk about her dad in this house. This house, into which he'd never once been welcomed. She stared at her hands. Her fingers had twisted themselves awkwardly together. She forced them to separate and hang empty at her sides. "I heard him play in a club when I was six." The memory flooded her, as immediate as ever, and she tilted her head back, blinking to clear her eyes. "He was amazing. His music was like honey on fire. Lick-your-fingers sweet and white-hot at the same time."

"I'm envious."

She looked at Spencer. Weight resting on one hip, hands resting in his pockets, he stood rooted in one place, as if he would stand there until the world split into a million pieces and time stopped, just to listen to her speak. That she felt comfortable doing so was the surprise.

"She never let him set foot in this house. Not once," she said. The many-paned windows looking out onto the sweep of the snow-covered front lawn were a step away. She stroked the velvet nap of the heavy, floor-length drapes. She meant her laugh to be harsh. It wasn't. "You'd think the music would have been something they had in common."

The sharp edges of the lead mullions created a diamond pattern that wavered before her. Stupid tears. She wondered if she could blame it on PMS, which sometimes made her weepy at the most ridiculous moments. A knuckle under her lashes erased any trace of moisture before she faced the room, and Spencer, again.

"Wanna show me the rest of the house?" She brushed past the intimate moment as if it hadn't occurred. Something that was becoming a habit with her and this man. Neither of them had spoken a word about the kiss they'd shared earlier. And it had been much more than just a kiss, if she was honest.

She started to leave the room. A sharp tug at her elbow spun her around.

"Not this time." Spencer stood over her. He gripped her shoulders and gave her a little shake. "I can see what you're doing, what you're thinking, as if I were inside your head, Addy. Do you think I don't notice it? How you shut down completely as soon as you catch yourself talking to me like a normal human being?"

Tearing herself out of his hands, she left the room.

"You can just stay out of my head," she said, throwing the words over her shoulder.

"Your great-aunt gave up her music." He followed her into the hall entryway. The man couldn't let a damn thing go without having the last word. She ignored him.

He kept talking.

"I don't know why she did it, but whatever her reasons were, she never played again. Even here, in her own home, she kept this room closed up." She heard him sigh. Watched her fingertips as they skated over the checkerboard inlay of a small table against the wall.

"Maybe she was afraid of your father—if not for herself, then for what he might represent for your mother."

This was a bit much. No one should make excuses for her great-aunt's actions. No one could.

"And maybe it just wasn't proper." She looked him straight in the eye. Listen up, buddy. "Her niece got herself pregnant by a guy who had to work for a living, a musician who played in bars, not symphony halls. Instead of the grand society wedding, there was a quick ceremony at City Hall. And instead of gossiping proudly about the match with all her rich friends, Great-Aunt Adeline pretended it never happened. That my parents simply didn't exist."

"You may find this hard to believe—" he was angry now, she could see, blue eyes narrowed and alive with energy, both hands open in the air as if he'd like to reach out and strangle her "—but to a woman like your great-aunt, what was *proper,* as you put it, was important. She grew up in a different world and she believed she'd been taught what was right."

"Still with the excuses," she said and threw her hands up. "You know what I was taught by my parents, Reed?" She pointed a finger at him, stopped herself from poking him with it. "That nothing matters more than love. What you love. Who you love. That's it. All that counts in this life."

Before he could open his mouth, she raised her hands in surrender.

"Listen, Reed." She shut her mouth and shrugged, caught without words for a moment. She went with the first sentence that floated to the surface. "I don't want to fight with you."

He looked blank for a moment and then began what she could only describe as laughing his ass off. After a moment, she grinned with him.

"Contrary to appearances," she admitted. He might be a bit stiff and spend way too much money on his wardrobe, but at least the guy had a sense of humor. "It's midnight. I've got to get up in five hours, less if I want to dig out my truck instead of calling a cab, and I'm already tired at the thought. So why don't you give me the ten-cent tour of this house that'll never be mine and we'll call it a night."

"All right." He gave in gracefully and cupped his hand around her elbow to guide her up the stairs. She shrugged off his hand. "But next time you won't get off so easy."

"Yeah, well, next time I won't fall for the 'why don't you sit down in front of the nice warm fire and curl up in this blanket while I read you really boring legal documents' trick." She made sure not to stomp up the stairs, so he would know she was kidding.

"Hey, some tricks only work once." She whipped her head around to find him grinning at her, and then stumbled up the next step and cursed. "I'm kidding. It's called humor. When jokes are exchanged between two friends."

"Don't push it, Reed." She stopped at the top of the stairs and stared down at him. "Let's see how friendly you think I am when I come banging on your door at five in the morning, wanting you to help me shovel a path to the street."

"That's what friends are for, right?"

"I'd bet most of your friends just pick up the phone and call for their drivers to pull the limo around."

"Don't be petty. It doesn't suit you." He brushed his hands against her hips to move her out of his way. She felt each fingertip like a small electric shock and then her stomach slid into that slow, rolling loop that she was coming to expect whenever he touched her. "Follow me. I'll make this quick."

"You don't know what suits me," she muttered, keeping her voice low enough to avoid the inevitable comeback if he heard her. Spencer was striding down the hall in front of her, pointing right and left like an air traffic controller and calling out information.

There were six rooms on the second floor. Two bedrooms, each with its own bath, thanks to someone in her family tree who'd had a fondness for extensive indoor plumbing, and two suites at diagonally opposite ends of the floor. Each suite had a master-size bedroom and bathroom and another attached room, which in one suite had been made into an office and in the other, an artist's studio.

"I don't know who the artist was, but it's a good space," Spencer said, walking her through the bedroom of that suite and into the connecting room. "Lots of light. Plenty of room if someone wanted to set up a drafting table for construction plans, say." He knew better than to look at her with that leading statement.

"Shut up, Reed," she answered, no real malice in her voice. She stood in the middle of the open room—no curtains on these windows to block the southern light—and knew that she wanted this house. She thought of her cozy but cramped one-bedroom apartment, a place that she didn't own and that could be taken from her in a month if her building went condo, and then craved this house.

She'd been here for six hours, had hated the very thought of the place and the woman who had lived here, and yet she felt the timbers of the floors and the plaster of the walls settling into her bones with a rightness that scared her.

It was all impossible.

"Very nice," she said, forcing her voice to be steady, pretending all was normal. "I'm sure the charity Great-Aunt Adeline named will be thrilled to receive it when I don't meet the terms."

"Don't make up your mind yet, Addy."

He was watching her, she knew, and when she turned to him, she also knew he would read the unhappiness in her eyes. He stood with his hands in his pockets, sleeves unrolled but unbuttoned, cuffs hanging open around his wrists. Her sadness made her honest.

"It's not a matter of deciding anything and you know it. The fact is, I'm not married, and don't see myself strolling down the aisle anytime soon."

His words were measured. "You have some time to fulfill the requirements of the will."

"One year." She walked back into the bedroom and dropped onto the edge of the bed. "Don't get me wrong. I'm sure the average guy would just as soon marry me as watch the Bears play Monday Night Football, but I just don't see this happening."

He'd followed her into the bedroom and now moved as if to sit down on the bed. Her look stopped him while he was still a yard away. He was frowning at her.

Great, now she felt guilty. Years on construction sites might have made her a little rough around the edges, but she didn't usually go around trying to make people feel bad.

"Don't worry about it, Reed. Two days ago, I didn't know this place existed. So it's not like I'm really losing anything. I never had it to begin with." Time to change the subject. "Which room is yours?"

"At the other end of the hall. The one with the office."

She'd peeked in the door to each room, something she could now kick herself for as the image snaked its way into her mind of Reed's naked torso wrapped in navy sheets, one tanned arm curled beneath his head, eyes closed in deep slumber. She shook her head, hoping the rattling of her brains would dispel the picture, and stood up.

"Then this room is perfect for me." She held out a hand to him. "Thanks for the hospitality. See you in the morning."

Deep-ocean glints in his eyes kept thoughts of navy blue sheets front and center in her imagination as he took her hand and shook it solemnly before leaving the room.

At the threshold he paused, one hand on the doorknob, and knocked her back onto the edge of the bed with a look.

"I may be at the other end of the hall, Addy, but the doors don't lock."

The last thing she saw before he tugged the door shut behind him was his wink.

She opened her mouth and then snapped it shut. Trying for the last word in this situation was *not* a good idea. After all, she was about to slide between the sheets of a bed in a house shared only by a man who'd already kissed her senses into oblivion once this evening.

Provoking him into trying again was not the sane choice.

But part of her wanted to.

After washing up, Addy snapped off all the lights in the room except for the warming, colorful glow of the stained-glass lamp on the night table, and climbed into bed, enjoying the feel of the soft, worn cotton sheets on her bare skin. Tugging on the lamp's chain, she plunged the room into darkness and wrapped the down quilt around her shoulders, listening to the quiet sounds of an old house settling into sleep. She would be happy to do the same.

Twenty minutes later, she gave up and turned the light back on. She'd left the pile of legal documents on the night table and grabbed them now, hoping to bore herself into falling asleep.

Or at least to distract herself from the idea of the two unlocked doors between her and the sleeping Spencer Reed of the surprisingly muscular frame.

If sleep was what she'd hoped for, she'd made the wrong choice in reading her great-aunt's will, she thought with frustration a wakeful hour later. Going over the specific details of Adeline's bequest did nothing but make her angry. Make her wish she had her great-aunt standing in front of her so she could shake some sense into the crazy woman.

"This is ridiculous!" Pages flew across the room and scattered in swirls like gusts of giant snowflakes. "Does she think I'm living in a damn gothic romance novel? Crazy witch!"

She'd read the will for the first time and told herself that it was sheer curiosity that kept her going past the first page. But at two in the morning, the only soul awake in a quiet house, Addy admitted to herself that she'd hoped…hoped to come across some loophole, some way out that would let her keep this house. Because she wanted it. Wanted it with a passion that she knew came from years of feeling the monetary tightrope wobble beneath her feet as a child.

When she was eleven years old, she knew how to balance a checkbook. How to deposit her mother's meager paychecks and write out payments for the monthly bills, leaving them waiting on the kitchen table for her mother's signature when she came home from another late shift at the hospital. She knew each month how close to the edge her family came, how each time one of her siblings outgrew a pair of gym shoes, paying the rent became a juggling act.

When her high school friends had spun fantasies about winning the lottery and going on shopping sprees, she'd always said the same thing: "I'd buy a house." *So no one could take it away,* were the unspoken words that echoed in her mind each time.

And now here she was, her childhood fantasy dropped into her lap as if a fairy godmother had waved her wand and granted her fondest wish.

And she couldn't keep it.

Loopholes. She should have known better. Should have known that an attorney like Reed wouldn't allow any such laxity in a document he'd drafted. Even knowing he'd been obligated to do so, that he hadn't even known who she was at the time, Addy couldn't help resenting him just a little bit.

What kind of lawyer let his client write up something as ridiculous as this antiquated blackmail trap of a will?

The light didn't get any brighter outside of her windows. The sun wouldn't creep over the winter horizon until after she'd arrived at her office. But by four in the morning, having counted the number of rose clusters on the floral wallpaper on the facing wall—three hundred and twenty-six, thank you very much—she had to get out of that house.

She dressed without making a sound. Crept down the stairs and stopped for a moment to rip a sheet of paper out of her site notebook and scribble a note, which she left on the marble-topped table by the front door.

She heard the *whuff* of rough breathing and the creak of the floorboards at the same moment.

"Jesus, Elwood," she gusted, and the dog shoved a cold nose into her palm. "I thought you were a cat burglar." She scratched the dog roughly behind the ears as he leaned heavily against her leg. "You be quiet now."

She patted him one last time and then let herself silently out the front door. Trudging a path through the newly pristine snow, she ignored the cold and refused to look back at the house she felt looming behind her.

It was a dream of a house, meant for a dreamlike fantasy life. But that wasn't her life. And it was time to head into work.

Spencer stood at the window, watching Addy's bundled form stride determinedly through the drifts and out the front gate. At least she wouldn't have to battle ice and snow before hitting the road. He'd gone outside nearly an hour before and cleaned off her truck, clearing enough snow to make sure she could get going this morning with ease.

He'd known, somehow, that she wouldn't come and ask him to help her, no matter what she'd threatened. If there was one thing he'd figured out about this woman, it was that she'd as soon chew her own hand off before sticking it out to ask for help.

He wasn't surprised either that she'd left without waiting for morning or breakfast or to say goodbye. The naked look of desire in her eyes as she'd wandered from room to room hadn't been as successfully shuttered as the rest of her emotions. It would hurt her to stay and wish for something she couldn't have.

A woman like Addy Tyler would rather walk out into the cold of a freezing morning and face her reality than sit in a cozy bed dreaming.

Spencer jogged down the staircase and headed to the kitchen. He was up; might as well get the coffee brewing.

A flutter of white caught his eye. He hadn't expected a note.

You can't always get what you want. Isn't that what the Stones sang? You're a good host, Reed. Tell the charity I wish them well with the house.
Addy

He blinked and found the note crumpled in his fist. The desire to go back in time to his conversations with Adeline and voice some of the doubts he'd felt but kept silent about came near to overwhelming him.

She might drive him crazy with her stubbornness and her never-ending rudeness and baiting of him, but he knew one thing: Addy Tyler deserved this house. If only so she could exorcise her own ghosts.

Not one to dwell in anger, Spencer headed back toward the kitchen. By the time his steps had planted him in front of the coffeemaker, he had his cell phone in hand.

In the end, he decided that four in the morning was a little too early to be making the phone call he'd planned and settled down at the kitchen table with some contracts in need of line edits.

When the clock over the stove ticked onto seven o'clock, however, he punched in the number he'd pulled from his handheld organizer.

"I hope I'm not waking you, Mrs. Tyler. But I wanted to introduce myself to you as soon as possible and discuss a few matters important to us both."

"My name is Spencer Reed, and I'm going to be getting married to your daughter Addy."

Four

To say that her family didn't take her news well would be putting it mildly.

And that was before she found out about the bombshell dropped on her mother by Mr. Take-Charge Attorney-at-Law.

Mr. Stick His Nose In Where It Wasn't Wanted was more like it.

"I'm not marrying your buddy Spike!" she shouted at last and whipped a couch pillow at her brother's big, fat, incredibly stupid head.

He ducked in his recliner and snagged the pillow in midflight, rescuing several framed pictures on the wall behind him. "Wait a second!" He made a T with his hands, the quarterback calling for a thirty-second time-out in the last minute of the big game. "Not for *real*. What do you think I am, crazy? Just one of those—what do they call 'em—*marriage of convenience* things."

"First of all, you *are* crazy. That's a given," put in her sister Sarah, curled up at the far end of the couch with a book in her lap and her long, straight hair in a neat ponytail. When their brother launched the abused couch pillow at her, she grabbed it one-handed and tucked it under her knees, sticking out her tongue at him when he pouted at the end of the fun. "Weren't you paying attention? Addy's got to live with her husband in that house for six months. You want her to share rooms with Spike?"

"There is something about a man almost entirely covered with tattoos." This, dreamily, from Maxie, sitting on the floor at Sarah's side. Addy's youngest sister was looking very *Breakfast at Tiffany's* today, with her short, curly hair pinned ruthlessly into control, a tailored black-and-white dress and matching wide-brimmed hat. Oversize black sunglasses perched on the coffee table next to her.

"Yeah, something that says he's lost his mind." Addy looked for a pillow to throw. They were all under someone else's control. She settled for sticking out her tongue at her baby sister. "That's enough out of you, Audrey Hepburn."

Maxie's wide grin told her she'd guessed correctly at the day's costume. And why was her brother still babbling on?

"…just saying, if you offered him five grand, he'd sleep in the garage for six months. No problem."

Her brother's hopeful, handsome grin almost made her smile, but she kept her face straight and her voice firm. "I'm not marrying Spike just so he can pay you back the money you loaned him to buy that Harley. That was your dumb decision, not mine." At the sudden clamor of voices, she ducked her head and threw her hands in the air. "Tsst! Enough! I'm not going to scam my way into this thing. I'm not getting married and that's that."

She collapsed onto the couch and flung a bent arm over her face. Scenes with her family were always such a drama. Although each person was sane on his or her own, put them all in one room and they were certifiable.

"That's not what I heard." Her mother's voice from the living room doorway drew all of their attention. She lifted a hot-pink apron over her head, revealing a trim black pantsuit. "Dinner in ten." She left the room.

"What's not what you heard?" Addy could hear the whine in her own voice. The chaos was getting out of hand when her mom joined in. The doorbell rang. "And who's at the door? Mom?"

"I'll get it," Maxie said, bouncing up from her cross-legged seat as only a twenty-year-old girl could do and running to the foyer. They could hear her voice as she opened the door. "Hi! Who are you?"

"I'm your dinner guest. Nice hat."

"Thanks! Come on in."

But Addy had recognized that voice. She should. She heard it every time her brain stopped racing around in circles of thought. *Don't make up your mind yet, Addy.*

She leaped up off the couch and braced herself in the doorway to the front hall, hands clutching the door frame.

"What the hell are you doing here, Reed?" Before he could answer, she was shouting for her mother, feeling suddenly like a teenager again. Completely out of control.

Her mom, who disliked people who rang doorbells at the dinner hour, stepped calmly into the foyer, finished wiping her palms on a dish towel and then extended a hand in welcome to the man standing in the open front doorway with laughter in his eyes.

"Welcome to my home, Mr. Reed," she said as they shook hands. "Maxie, sweetie, close the door. May I take your coat?"

"What!"

"Call me Spencer, Mrs. Tyler," the traitorous man said, shrugging out of his coat and passing it to Sarah, who hung it in the hall closet. "Thank you for inviting me to dinner tonight."

"What!"

"I like to have the whole family together at meals, Spencer. And, please, call me Susannah. Would you care for a glass of wine?"

Addy stared openmouthed as Spencer Reed followed her mother toward the back of the house, the two chatting pleasantly as if they'd had dinner together once a week for the last decade. Her siblings took one look at her, shrugged in unison and trooped off to find out who the stranger was and join the fun.

Left alone in the chilly foyer, feeling cold water seep into her socks from the puddle she'd stepped in—a puddle no doubt left by Reed's snow-crusted shoes; the man was completely without consideration for others—Addy waited for the world to stop tilting underneath her.

"What the hell is going on here?"

The whole family together?

The moment she set foot in the dining room, the barrage of voices, some directed at her, some not, hit her like a blow to the solar plexus. Bracing herself, she ignored everyone and made a beeline for Reed, who was about to sit down.

She grabbed his arm and yanked him out of his chair.

Ignoring all protests, including her mother's—she'd pay for that one later—she dragged him back down the hall.

"What are you doing here?" she hissed at him, trying to keep her voice down.

He leaned against the wall, looking completely at his ease. The fact that she could recognize his scent—warm vanilla and leather—irritated her. It made her hungry.

"Your mother and I thought it would be a good time for me to get to know your family," he said as if it were the most natural thing in the world.

"And when did you two decide this?"

"When I called her this morning," came the answer. She could see him trying to hold back the smile now. His mouth stayed solemn but his eyes were a dead giveaway. "Your hair sure does fly all over the place." He reached out a hand and tucked a riotous curl behind her ear.

She slapped him away. "Stop touching me. Why were you calling my mother?"

"I know it's old-fashioned, but I still believe in asking the girl's parents for permission before you marry her."

"Are you crazy?" All thoughts of keeping quiet went right

out the window as she bellowed at him. "You told my mother we're getting married?"

"Keep your cool, Addy."

She could have punched him right in the face for leaning there, calm and poised, arms crossed loosely on his chest.

"Screw my cool!" She stamped her foot and knew she was acting like a five-year-old. It was beyond her control. Spencer stood up straight and took a step toward her. "Who do you think you are?" She felt crowded and pushed him back, hard. Liked it, and pushed him again. "My knight in goddamn shining armor?"

Her breath was heaving in her chest. She was appalled by her lack of control but couldn't seem to rein in her fury.

"It's a simple solution to a difficult problem."

He was not helping.

And he was so damn cute in those glasses.

"Adeline Tyler." Ignoring her mother twice was not an option. She turned to face the stern glance. "Spencer is our guest. We do not yell at our guests. And the rest of your family is ready to eat."

Addy nodded. Plastering a smile on her face, she gestured for Spencer to proceed before her. Safely hidden behind his suit-coated back, she dropped the fake enthusiasm.

"We'll finish this later, you conniving weasel."

He turned and grabbed her by the elbows, yanking her up against his body before she could react. His eyes glittered and there wasn't a hint of cuteness about him as he ground a hard, brief kiss against her stunned mouth.

"We certainly will, you stubborn witch."

Dinner was hell.

Only her mother's stern edict that any and all interrogations under hot lights be postponed until after the meal kept her siblings in check. Addy, stuck sitting across from the archfiend himself, kept her eyes away from him and her mouth shut.

After dinner, she made a move to corner Spencer, only to

watch him get spirited away by her two sisters on a tour of the house, her brother following two steps behind them with a dark look. Addy was stuck clearing the table with her mother.

In the kitchen, loading the dishwasher, she had only one sentence for the woman she loved more than life itself.

"I'm not marrying him and I don't want to hear another word about it."

"Whatever you say, sweetie." Her mother scraped plates before handing them along. "Just take it outside before you start yelling at him again."

Minutes later, she kissed her mom on the cheek, got a hug in return and went to hunt down her man.

She found them all in the living room.

"Everyone out." She speared one set of eyes with a cold look. "Except me?"

"Except you."

Her siblings left obediently, but not before she caught a wordless exchange between the two men in the room that boded more conversation between them later.

Remain calm. She chanted the words in her head like a silent mantra.

"I understand what you're trying to do here, Reed," she began calmly, "but, frankly, I'd rather marry Spike."

"Spike? Maybe your great-aunt was right to worry about you." His brow wrinkled and he ran a hand through his hair, loosening blond waves. "Is that your boyfriend?"

"Hardly." As she stood there, a dozen questions and confusions battled for first place in her mind. "It's a long story."

He sank gracefully onto the faded couch, looking more comfortable than a man in what was undoubtedly a two-thousand-dollar suit had a right to look. "I'm not going anywhere. And you're better off if I can vouch for your mental stability. Tell me a story."

She marched to the hall closet and grabbed his overcoat.

"No stories," she said and tossed the coat onto the couch next to him. "Get out."

He crossed a leg over one knee and draped his arm across the back of the sofa. And waited.

Two could play at that game, she thought. She turned her back on him and walked over to the window onto the street. Leaning against the cold glass, she stared out at the quiet houses across the road and cleared her mind of all thoughts of Spencer Reed and his ridiculous proposal.

Not that he'd even proposed to her.

Stop it, she berated herself. Look at the houses. The Jansens look as though they're putting on an addition, isn't that nice?

Thirty seconds later, she admitted that she wasn't going to win this battle. Her only triumph was that she managed to keep her back to him when she spoke.

"Can't you get disbarred for this? It must be some kind of conflict of interest."

"Probably." His voice was rich with amusement. She felt it curling around her like the touch of his fingers in her hair. "I'm willing to try and figure a way around it."

"Why?"

"Maybe I thought you looked right in your great-aunt's house. Like you belonged there."

She snorted in disbelief. "You look like you belong there way more than I do." Her own words sparked a tiny candle flame of suspicion in her. She wanted a reason to suspect his motives. Needed it. The suspicion grew.

Fancy clothes. Fancy car. Run-down office. Living at a client's house. Was she missing the obvious here?

"Is this a con?" She whirled around and stared at him. He hadn't moved from his seat. "What, you dress rich to cover up the fact that you're broke and then try to scam your way into marrying me to get your hands on my great-aunt's house?"

Complete silence.

She watched him as he stood up and shrugged into his coat. He pulled leather gloves from his pockets and tugged them onto his hands. Then he walked past her to the front door.

"Oh, so now you're leaving?"

"No. *We're* leaving. Get your coat."

"I'm not going anywhere with you," she sputtered at the back of his head.

"Susannah, I'll bring Addy back in half an hour," he called out before turning to stare at her. His lips pressed together in a tight line as he looked at her as if she were something he'd accidentally stepped in and then scraped off the bottom of his shoe.

"Okay, Spencer. Lovely meeting you this evening," came her mother's voice in return. The casual acceptance stung.

"Get your coat."

She obeyed. The sinking suspicion that she'd let her fear of the situation talk her mouth into writing a check of accusation she didn't want to cash was crystallizing in her stomach.

The air outside was bitterly cold, and ice sheeted the sidewalk where salt hadn't been spread. He didn't take her arm to steady her, or even look at her as she followed him to his car. Ten steps away, the BMW beeped, clicked, blinked on lights and purred to life with a low rumble.

"Nice car," she muttered as he opened the passenger-side door for her.

"Shut up." He slammed the door shut as soon as she swung her legs in.

How do I get myself into these situations? she wondered. What happened to "remain calm"?

The vents were already blowing warm air across her cheeks, but she felt ice radiating off Spencer as he slid into the driver's seat. She ventured to speak.

"Listen, maybe I jumped the gun—"

"Not a word, Addy."

They pulled away from the curb in one smooth acceleration. He drove quickly but carefully through the quiet streets. She clasped her hands in her lap, feeling like a schoolgirl waiting outside the principal's office door, and stared out the windshield.

Ten minutes later, they were in Lincoln Park, the north

side's high-rent district, on one of the main streets where commercial and retail spaces mixed with the occasional residential building. He pulled over in a loading zone and parked, leaving the engine running.

When he got out of the car and walked around to her side, she didn't wait for him. She stepped out onto the sidewalk and shut the door behind her, just in time to be pushed by Spencer up to the edge of a temporary construction fence surrounding the building they'd parked in front of. Scaffolding and blue tarp hid most of the three-story gray-stone building from sight.

A building like that would go for two million in this neighborhood, she knew, easy.

His body was a brick wall behind her. He clamped one hand on her shoulder, fingers tight through her winter coat, and with the other forced her chin up until she stared at the building in front on her. His voice vibrated with tension like a tightly twisted rope, two seconds from snapping.

"I own this building. My office will be on the ground floor, my home on the top two. I'll have a copy of the deed sent to your office by messenger tomorrow morning."

If you're going to screw up, do it in a big way, she'd always said. Or at least, she'd be saying it from now on.

When he didn't continue, only dropped his hand from her chin to rest it on her other shoulder, more gently now, she opened her mouth.

"My turn to speak?" She tried but couldn't keep a touch of asperity from her words.

Unbelievably, she thought he laughed behind her. "I've not noticed you waiting for turns so far."

She twisted in his grasp until she faced him. Tilting her head back to look him in the eye, she was excruciatingly aware of how close their mouths were. Time to act like a grown-up.

"I'm sorry. What I said was rude and uncalled for and I knew it wasn't true when I said it." Being a grown-up sucked.

Their faces were close enough that his breath warmed her

cheek when he spoke. He'd kept his hands on her as she'd turned, and she found that her own hands rested on his forearms as she looked steadily at him.

"Then why did you?"

She shrugged. "I don't know. Somehow you just bring out the *West Side Story* in me."

This time he did laugh. His smile revealed a dimple in one sharply planed cheek.

"Ready to rumble at a moment's notice?"

"Something like that." She looked away. This was crazy. The occasional car hissed past through the slush-covered street, and she was about two seconds from kissing this man she'd only just apologized to for calling a con artist. She looked back. "I really am sorry, Reed."

"One of these times, you're going to call me by my first name," he said, and then his mouth was on hers and she was glad he hadn't made her kiss him first. Without a thought, her hands slid up his arms until her gloved fingers pressed fiercely on the back of his neck as her mouth opened to him. She breathed his breath and nipped at his lip and her need poured from her into his kiss.

The fence swayed a little behind her as they stumbled up against it and a passing car honked at them, but every sensation outside of the kiss came to her as if from miles away. The taste of his mouth, still sweet from dessert. The pressure of his hand locked onto her hip. The storm of this kiss, raging between them, was all she could feel.

His other hand fisted in her hair, tugging her head deliciously back until her bare throat was exposed to the cold night air and the heat of his lips and tongue skating down the column of her neck. Even with her eyes closed, she could see the stars in the black night above her.

The shock of ice in her pants had her jerking away from the embrace with a sudden start.

"Hey, now!"

Spencer had managed to unbutton her coat and snake his

hands inside and up under her shirt, something she hadn't minded at all at the time. But now, with snow from his gloves and the fence and the world in general sliding south of her waistline, she was considerably less enthusiastic.

"Ice. Ice in pants," she said, hopping in a circle and trying to scoop out the snow wedged in her pants with two curled fingers. She only managed to push it in farther. "Ai yi yi, so cold." She gave up. Turning her back on Spencer, she unzipped her pants, gasped at the smack of cold air on her skin and finally managed to rid herself of the chilly clumps. Struggling with gloved fingers to pull her zipper back up, she heard what sounded suspiciously like choking coming from behind her.

"I swear to God, if you're laughing, Reed, you're gonna know exactly what this feels like in about two seconds."

Before she could turn around, his arms were around her, bundling her up in an enormous hug. His lips were cold against her ear as he whispered, laughter in his voice.

"I wouldn't dare."

In a second, he had her spun around and pressed up against the side of his car.

"Where were we?"

She pressed her palms firmly against his chest and reared her head back out of reach.

"We were making a big mistake, that's where we were."

Tugging on her scarf, he tried to pull her closer. "No, no, no. I'm the sensible one." He leaned his hips against hers and the focus of her entire body shot south. "You're the one who can't control her impulses."

"You're the attorney," she said, keeping away from his mouth and wondering where this sudden sense of responsibility had sprung from. "I'm the client."

"Your great-aunt was my client."

"Same difference."

"Not hardly." But he gave in, dropping his hands and pausing only to press his forehead against hers. She felt him take a couple of deep breaths. "But I see your point."

Stepping out of his embrace, she put her hand on the car door and opened it. "Come on, let's go." After she slid into her seat, he pushed the door softly shut. He stood next to the car, motionless for a little while, before walking around it and getting in. He was shaking his head, but didn't say anything.

She waited until they'd arrived back at her mother's house, double-parking next to her truck. After a moment of silence, she scooched around in her seat until she was facing him, one arm braced on her seat, the other on the dash.

"Look, Reed," she began, and then stopped. She didn't want to be abrupt now. The words mattered because she knew she was right. "I appreciate the fact that you want to help. Really, I do. But this isn't going to work."

His face was shadowed. "Which part of it?"

She understood immediately. His offer to marry her and what happened between them every time they got within two feet of each other were separate things. Unfortunately.

"Any of it."

His exhale echoed her own. "I don't want you to give up on your great-aunt's house, Addy."

"I'm not." She laughed at herself and caught his answering smile. "I didn't want to scam my way into her inheritance at first, but I'll admit it now—I've changed my mind. If Great-Aunt Adeline wanted to put some crazy rules in her will, I'm willing to be a little crazy in turn."

He reached a hand over and squeezed her knee. "That shouldn't be too hard."

Good, they were back to teasing insults. She was comfortable with that. "My insanity only goes so far. I'll find someone to marry, but it'll be someone I'm not so..." She drifted off into silence.

His hand slid higher up her thigh. She felt every molecule in her body vibrate with renewed tension and caught her breath on a sharp inhale.

"So instantly attracted to?" He bared white teeth in a sudden grin.

"It may surprise you to hear this, Reed, but I don't hop in-to bed with every guy I'm attracted to, much less marry them." She popped the door open and jumped out of the car. She'd learned her lesson about staying near him when she felt like this. He leaned over the console between the seats to keep her in his sight.

"It wouldn't surprise me at all." He laughed shortly. "Half of them are probably running scared after you give them a tongue-lashing that reminds them of their mothers."

"Flatterer."

"Just promise me that you won't do anything sudden, Ad-dy." His voice was abruptly serious and his gaze locked on hers, extracting a promise she didn't want to give. "Let me know if you decide to do something and then give yourself twenty-four hours to think about it, okay? You've got some time here."

She'd just turned his offer down flat and he was still try-ing to look out for her. A sweet warmth stole over her. She ducked her head back in the car and pressed a quick, cold kiss to his cheek.

"You're a good man, Spencer Reed," she whispered in his ear and felt his hand brush over her hair like an angel's kiss.

She shut the car door and sprinted up the walk to her moth-er's door. Time to say goodbye before heading home. On the porch, she turned and looked back at his dark form sitting still in the car. He raised one hand in a brief farewell and drove away while she watched him.

A good man.

Two weeks later, Addy would have paid a thousand dol-lars for a rewind button on life that let her go back to that mo-ment outside the car, just so she could lunge back in the door and smack him silly.

A good man. Bah. A dirty-dealing, underhanded sneak was more like it. She should have known better than to think Spencer Reed was looking out for her. Too trusting, that's what she was.

The man was driving her batty. Another two weeks of this nonsense and she'd be *asking* for the straitjacket and the keys to the padded room.

All because she'd taken him at his word. Foolish girl.

Three days after the dinner at her mom's house, Addy had left a message on Spencer's voice mail at work. She'd called after midnight, hoping that even an obvious workaholic like him would have left the office by then. Keeping it brief, she'd simply told him that she'd made arrangements with one of her brother's co-workers for a marriage that would end amicably in divorce, after the appropriate time stipulated in her great-aunt's will.

The part she came to regret was that she'd mentioned the man's name.

At quarter to five the next evening, a messenger had arrived at her office bearing a slim envelope with two sheets of paper. The first was a note from Spencer.

The second page was a rap sheet.

Maybe you'd better think twice about this guy. I don't think Susannah would approve of you marrying someone with a record, even temporarily.
Spencer

After calling up her brother to read him the riot act and probably getting the guy fired to boot, she'd reluctantly decided to look elsewhere. Although the temptation to go ahead just to spite her self-appointed guardian angel was strong.

She wasn't that stubborn, though, so she'd rejoined the search. At that point, she'd even felt a little gratitude toward Spencer. He obviously cared what happened to her.

But when she left her next message, she was careful to be deliberately vague about her new choice. No sense letting the man think she wanted him to vet every prospective groom.

She should have known better. Who knew what a busybody a guy with a law degree could be? It turned out that he called up her mother and pried the name of the latest man out of her.

This time, his note arrived with a videocassette wrapped in brown paper.

Moving from ex-convicts to former stars of pornographic films is not necessarily a step in the right direction. Are you sure you're a good judge of character? Although the movie did get four stars in Adult Video Monthly.
Spencer

Drat the man. She didn't need an angel. Just someone willing to share a house and a marriage license for a while in exchange for some cash. On the other hand, the porn-star thing was a little creepy.

At this point, she stopped leaving him messages. The damage, however, had been done. After hearing about her first two unbelievably poor choices, her family conspired behind her back to work with Spencer. Despite her stern commands to the contrary, she found out that they'd started calling him up and asking him to run background checks.

Two weeks of this madness was enough.

She banged with a fist on his office door, a crumpled slip of paper sticking out between her clenched fingers, and hollered his name.

"Reed! Get your butt out here!"

She heard his measured tread approaching the door and waited for him, one foot tapping like a jackhammer on the cement stoop. As the door swung open, she held the latest note between both hands and snapped it open with a crinkling of wrinkled paper.

"What is this supposed to mean?" she demanded.

"Good evening to you, too, Addy," he said and gestured for her to enter. When she ignored him, he glanced at the note. "I believe it says, 'You're kidding, right? Spencer.'"

"Don't avoid the question." She poked him in the chest with one finger. "What's wrong with Steve Henderson?"

"Not a thing," he said. The moment she let her smirk show, he opened his mouth again and she knew she'd triumphed too soon. "If you're into bigamy, that is."

"He's married?" Like a balloon popped by a pin, her shoulders slumped and her head sank. "Since when did it get so hard to find a good man to marry you for cash?"

"I couldn't tell you, but do you think we could continue this inside? I'm freezing here."

She looked him up and down and realized that he was standing in front of her in jeans, a casual white button-down shirt and bare feet. His hair was rumpled and his glasses dangled by a stem from his shirt pocket. She raised a questioning eyebrow.

"Friday is casual day around here, even for me. In, please?"

Stepping across the threshold, she gave him a wide berth as she passed. He closed the door behind her and the light in the hall dimmed further. Light shone from a door down the hall—his office, she presumed—but the rest of the building looked battened down for the weekend.

"I'd offer you coffee, but my assistant's gone for the night and she locks up everything except the decaf when she leaves. Claims I'm too irritable in the morning if I drink the real stuff all night long."

He strode off toward the light, assuming she'd follow. She considered staying put and just yelling but decided that wouldn't be dignified. She stalked after him.

In his office, she sank into the chair opposite his desk, swung both legs over one arm and dropped her head back over the other. She groaned aloud.

He said nothing.

"How am I supposed to pull this off if you shoot down every guy I dig up? You and my family. Traitors." She stared at the ceiling.

"We just want to make sure you don't end up hitched to a serial killer, or worse."

"Yeah, right."

"Besides, there's always another option, you know."

She rolled her head around and up to face him with great effort. With his head bent over a document, a too-long lock of blond hair falling in his eyes, Spencer studiously ignored her.

"I'm not marrying you."

"Whatever you say."

"And you need a haircut."

"Yes, dear."

"Oh, shut up."

Minutes ticked by. In the comfortable silence, she heard the clock on the wall tick off the time and the rustle of flipping pages as he read. Addy realized she was vaguely hungry and wondered when she'd last eaten.

After a while, she worked up the energy to leave. The process was quick, since she hadn't even removed her coat. She stood up, wincing at the puddle of dirty water her boots had dripped onto the linoleum floor.

"I'm outta here. I need to eat something. It's been about three days since my last meal." When he looked up at her, she could see the strain of overwork in the faint blue shadows beneath his eyes. "Don't worry, I'm not giving up. Maybe there's a gas station attendant taking a break from his career as a bank robber I can go propose to."

"If you wait a bit, I'll join you." He smiled and her heart tumbled a little bit. "In the meal, not the proposal."

"No, thanks." It felt as if she were kicking a puppy. But she was drawing a line here. "You're involved enough in my life as it is, right now, without us arguing over who picks up the check."

"Suit yourself."

At the door to the hall she paused, accustomed by now to his parting shots.

Sure enough.

"Don't do anything rash, Addy. We'll be watching."

"I bet," she muttered under her breath and left the building.

Valiantly resisting the temptation to head to a bar and start hitting up men for marital prospects, she drove home instead, stopping to pick up takeout at her local Chinese restaurant.

Sitting awake in bed at two in the morning, empty white cartons stacked high on her nightstand, she tried to focus on reading *Pride and Prejudice.* Her brain insisted on tumbling options one over the other like semiprecious stones in a gem polisher. There had to be a way around this problem. She was a smart woman. She'd passed four years of advanced math by the time she finished her graduate degree, for God's sake. She could figure out a way to fix this problem without Spencer Reed's help.

She woke up at dawn the next morning, still tired and with an MSG hangover. Even her dreams were conspiring against her, filled as they had been with erotic images of Spencer's hands racing over her body, strong caresses gentling in an instant to featherlight brushes against her skin. She was flushed and irritated, and rose with just one thought in her mind. The inescapable conclusion.

No time like the present. Sun's up and the day was wasting.

Banging on a door and calling Reed's name for the second time in twelve hours, she clenched her jaw and prepared to dig in.

He opened it, stained-glass panels shooting off rainbows in the early morning sun. He was barefoot again, but this time wearing only a pair of faded gray sweatpants slung low on his hips. Keeping her eyes off his bare torso, she shoved a box at him and watched him stumble with the unexpected weight.

His eyes were barely open. His mouth moved but no words managed to make their way from his sleep-befuddled brain into vocalization. So much the better. She'd start this off on her terms.

"We're going to lay down some ground rules here. But first, there's more where that came from in the truck."

She pushed past his still-silent form and headed up the staircase to her room.

Five

Coffee.

He needed coffee.

Pots of coffee. Gallons of cappuccino. Aquariums of espresso. Swimming pools of double café lattes. Or maybe just an intravenous needle hooked up to a bag of one hundred percent pure Colombian bliss.

Maybe he was still sleeping. He'd caught a glimpse of his alarm clock as he'd stumbled out of his bedroom to answer the incessant doorbell and simultaneous loud pounding on the door. If he wasn't hallucinating, which remained to be seen, it was six forty-five.

In the morning.

Saturday morning.

Coming to a vague consciousness, he found himself standing in his foyer. The chill air gusting through the open front door woke him up enough to kick it shut. Focus, Reed, he instructed his sleep-befuddled brain. Kitchen's thataway.

In the kitchen, he stood in the middle of the room wondering what he was supposed to be doing with this box, this very heavy box, in his arms. Finally, he dropped it. It landed with a solid thunk on the floor. Good. Didn't sound as if anything broke.

His feet were cold. He turned the oven up as far as it would go and opened the broiler door, letting hot air drift across the floor. Coffee. The damn machine was around here somewhere.

The coffeepot squatted on the counter, exactly where it had been since the first day he'd set foot in this house. He fumbled through the motions, grinding beans, filter, water, on button at last.

The thickening aroma of French roast was enough to start resuscitating his brain. At least enough for him to realize that heating the house via the oven was probably not the most efficient plan. Socks would maybe be a better idea. And a shirt; it was chilly down here.

He stumbled back upstairs and into his room, spotting his unmade bed with the pleasure of a treasure hunter finding the lost diamond. "Ahh, mine." He stopped to pull on socks and a sweatshirt even older and more frayed than the pants and then tumbled back into bed, winding a sheet around his shoulders and pushing his head under a pillow.

Two seconds later, something sharp poked him in the shoulder. He might have said *ouch* as he rolled over. Then something patted him on the butt and the mattress dipped as a huge weight landed on it and a cold, wet nose shoved itself into his armpit.

He threw one arm around the furry monster and wrestled it under control. "Elwood! Get down! Oof!"

Spencer sucked in air after his hundred-and-twenty-pound pooch used his stomach as a launching pad to jump to the floor. He coughed twice.

"Up and at 'em, lawyer boy." A viciously cheerful voice rang out from beside him. Memory started to filter in. Now he knew who'd lured the dog onto the bed. Pinching fingers grabbed one of his toes where they stuck out from under the covers, and yanked on them.

"Go 'way," he mumbled, renewing his grasp on the pillow over his head. Unable to fall asleep last night, he'd sat up over papers until his eyes had burned. By his best guess, he'd been asleep for about an hour and a half when this waking nightmare began.

She ripped the covers off him. Why he'd ever thought he was attracted to this woman was a complete mystery. She was the root of all evil.

And he was waking up. Dammit.

He cracked open one eye and was treated to the sight of Addy's butt sashaying out of his room. That was enough to bring him to full consciousness. If she wasn't a bad dream, then maybe he'd actually made that coffee.

Back in her new bedroom—for the next six months, at least—Addy closed the door and collapsed against it, the knob digging into the small of her back. Even fully dressed, the sight of him in bed was enough to spark visions of her crawling under the covers. Talk about rash. This was going to be harder than she'd imagined.

Taking a deep breath, she faced the door and squared her shoulders. Faint hearts and all that. She stepped back out into the hall.

"Where'd you put my files, Reed?" she started to shout before spotting him shuffling out of his room. His socks rasped faintly against the short pile of the faded runner on the floor. He headed down the stairs without glancing at her.

"Kitchen." He waved a hand toward the back of the house. "Box. Coffee."

"Not a morning person, huh?" she said, thumping down the stairs behind him in her heavy boots. At the bottom, she headed out the door to grab another load from her truck. When she came back in, Spencer was standing at the bottom of the stairs, her box in his arms and a coffee mug the size of a soup pot clutched precariously in two fingers.

"Great. Bring that up, will you?" At the door to her room, she dropped her own load and relieved him of his. Coffee mug lifted immediately and blue eyes blinked and peered at her over the rim as he gulped without stopping. She carried and kicked both boxes over to what she assumed was a closet door, and stacked them one on top of the other.

"Put your shoes on. There's more in the truck."

His eyes tracked her as she strode out of the room. Sleep-rough and slow, his voice called from behind her.

"Tell me Spike isn't waiting in the truck with the boxes. Please."

"Would I be asking for your help if he was?" Her words floated up to him from the foyer. "This was your idea, Reed. The least you can do is give me a hand."

This was how she asked for help? No wonder he felt like a Volkswagen flattened by a steamroller.

Although she lost him once midtask, only to find him re-caffeinating in the kitchen, she hadn't brought enough stuff to make the work last more than a half hour or so. Catching him paused at the bottom of the stairs, a box under one arm and his knee bracing another against the baluster while he sucked down more java, she scoffed.

"Why don't you just put a nipple on that thing and call it a pacifier?"

His eyes narrowed at her and he swigged back the dregs. "I've seen you swigging from your own cup all morning. I bet you twenty dollars that's not mountain spring water."

She flushed. "It's Diet Coke," she admitted, and then rushed to continue, "but I mix it half-and-half with caffeine-free. I'm trying to cut back."

"Me, too. Just not today."

After the last load was hauled up the stairs and deposited in her room, Spencer flung himself on her queen-size bed and groaned. Two seconds later, Elwood raced into the room and leapt up beside his master, turning in circles until he settled himself against Spencer's side. Addy wriggled out of her puffy down coat and slung it on a doorknob.

"I believe I mentioned some ground rules a while back," she

said as she started yanking clothes from boxes and shoving them in dresser drawers. She'd reorganize later. "Rule number one—neither you nor your dog is welcome in my bed."

"Have a heart, Addy. We're exhausted." He didn't move from his sprawl across the quilt. The dog just looked at her and drooled a little.

"You should get more exercise." Now wasn't the time for sympathy.

"She is a cruel, cruel woman, Elwood," he said, and dropped a consoling hand on the dog's head for a quick rub. Elwood grinned in agreement and drooled some more.

"Reed." A warning.

He rolled over onto his side and propped himself up on one elbow. His hair, mussed and sticking up in all directions from sleep, shone a deeper, darker gold in the rich, early morning light.

"You can list all the rules and regulations you want. That's not going to change the fact that every time we're in the same room for more than five minutes we want each other."

"Well, we're just going to have to be adults about it then, aren't we?" She snapped the wrinkles out of a sweater and refolded it, adding it to a growing stack on the dresser. "Want whatever you like. Just don't act on it." She slammed a drawer shut and reached for another box. "We'll be married on paper, but that's it. We do our own laundry, cook our own meals and stay out of each other's way as much as possible. And maybe we'll make it through this farce without killing each other."

He leaned over to stage-whisper in the dog's ear. "She's strict, too."

"This isn't a joke, Reed." She turned to face him and stopped short, seeing the three of them in this room for the first time and letting herself picture the next six months. The vision in her head had her sitting down suddenly on a box.

"I don't know what I was thinking. This is never going to work."

In a second, he'd bounced up off her bed and whistled for the dog to follow him.

"Sure it will. Don't quit now, when you've finally done the right thing." He ruffled her hair as an older brother would as he walked past her. "All kidding aside, I'm glad you're here. Just let me grab a quick shower and we can get going."

She held her head in her hands, unconvinced. *Going?*

"Where are we going?"

"To get married, of course." He stopped in the doorway, one hand gripping the frame, to throw her a quick grin. "Unless you want to drag this whole thing out, in which case I'd just as soon go back to bed for another three or four hours."

No, she didn't want to drag anything out. But, still—today? She'd be married to this man by the time the sun set? The vague twitches of nervousness in her stomach erupted into full-blown nausea at the thought. She was out of her ever-loving mind.

"Don't we need to get blood tests or something?" she asked, veering without any fun whatsoever between panic and the urge to run to her bathroom and throw up.

"Not in Wisconsin. We can be there in two hours." And with that last parting shot, he was gone. The dog followed but then raced back into the room a second later to give her one last sniff, followed by a wet welcome-to-our-home lick up the side of her face.

She scrubbed her cheek with her shirtsleeve. This was not how she'd ever pictured her life. Getting married to a relative stranger in Wisconsin on a couple hours' notice with dog slobber on her face.

"I owe you one, Great-Aunt Adeline." She spoke to the ceiling. "If either of us manages to make it to heaven, I'm going to somehow make you suffer for this."

On I-94 to Wisconsin, after a brief battle over the radio that ended in a compromise by settling on NPR in lieu of rock or classical, Addy settled into her seat and tried to relax. They'd already had skirmishes over several details since Spencer had emerged after his shower, steamy clean and smelling like heaven in a dress shirt and slacks. He'd suggested that she might want to change out of her jeans and black turtleneck. She'd claimed comfort first and won that one. Then Addy had suggested that she drive on the nuptial road trip. He'd claimed BMW comfort over Dodge Ram shock absorbers and won that one.

By the time she'd played along with the radio contestants on "Wait, Wait, Don't Tell Me" and tied or beaten them all, she realized that she had in fact relaxed a little. So had Spencer, apparently, since he was whistling some rippling brook of a melody as they sped down the highway in sleek fashion.

"Why are you so happy about all this?" she asked after another minute, kicking off her shoes and wedging her feet against the dash. When he frowned at her, she protested, "C'mon, I took my shoes off."

"Just be careful." He ducked his hand in his cuff and leaned forward to buff a faint scratch off the glove-compartment door.

"So, what gives?" She was pestering him for an answer she wasn't sure she really wanted but couldn't resist. Like scratching a mosquito bite until it bled. She'd trade him with an honest admission of her own. "I know I'm cranky enough for two people today. Why aren't you?"

"I told you before." He kept his eyes on the road. "You look right in that house, like you belong there. I just want to make sure that happens."

"Right. You're my guardian angel." She snorted out loud. A long, tangled curl caught at the corner of her mouth and she pulled the whole mass of her hair behind her head, securing it with a rubber band she found in her pocket.

"Or maybe I'm just taking a chance."

"On what?" She was genuinely curious.

"As much as you make me want to lock you up for your own safety, I'm oddly attracted to you." She saw his hands flex on the steering wheel and ignored the tremors that shot through her system. "You're an intelligent, interesting, beautiful woman. Maybe in six months' time, we'll decide that this wasn't so crazy after all. Good marriages have been founded on less promising terms."

"Can you actually be struck dead by lightning while traveling in a moving vehicle?" she wondered aloud. "Because that's about how likely I think your little scenario is."

"Well, I certainly haven't done a good job of finding the right woman by picking ones I actually like." A slight bitterness tinted his voice. "I may be better off with a woman I have to drag kicking and screaming to the altar than one who's racing to meet my checkbook there."

Now why should that sting? She supposed it was a backhanded compliment, contrasting her positively to a gold digger in his past. Still, she put on her sunglasses and pretended that she wasn't doing so to hide any hurt feelings in her eyes.

"Been burned before, have we?" She kept her tone careless.

"Haven't we all?" he answered shortly while flicking on a turn signal and easing into the right-hand lane.

"It's easier if you don't let them get too close," she answered without thinking, reciting what had been her motto ever since finding out that her grad-school boyfriend loved the career opportunities of a construction project more than he loved her. Ignoring Spencer's glance at her, she peered at the approaching rest area. "Perfect timing. I need to pee."

"It's really not necessary that you announce it." They pulled into a parking space. "Five minutes."

"What do you think I'm going to do? Go shopping?" She sprinted from the car to the building, leaping puddles of slush along the way. Spencer followed more slowly behind her.

By the time she got back to the car, he was already in his seat and napping. The sound of the door opening woke him and after one look at her, he turned the key in the ignition, shaking his head.

"So sue me," she said to his unspoken comment. "I like being a tourist." As they hit the road again, she plopped her new I Love Wisconsin baseball cap on her head, tugged the brim down over her eyes, leaned her seat all the way back and closed her eyes. She *had* offered to drive. And the conversation was getting way too serious for her.

He woke her up as they were turning into the courthouse parking lot. She ditched the cap and wrestled the sticky rubber band out of her hair, running her fingers through it for a moment in a futile attempt to get her curls under control. She considered slicking on a coat of lipstick and rejected the idea at once. Why pretend this was anything other than the final step of a business agreement?

One hour and a stream of words that flew by in a blur later, she was married.

Staring at the man who'd just sworn before what might have been a fish-and-game commissioner to love and cherish her until death—the official had insisted on "getting fancy with the lingo, folks"—she felt shaky and walked a little too close to the edge of crying. When Spencer simply looked at her after the official finished, and stuck out a hand, she blinked furiously and shook it.

"Congratulations," said the man, who'd clearly seen odder things.

"Thank you." They spoke in unison.

While Spencer finished up the paperwork, Addy stepped outside and dug her cell phone out of her backpack, taking a deep breath to collect herself. When her mother's voice mail picked up, she'd never been so happy to get a recording. There was no joy to be shared in a moment like this.

He joined her moments after she pressed the call-end button. They stood outside the courthouse and stared at the bleak winter scene in front of them. Neither spoke for a minute.

"I keep thinking they'd be so disappointed in me," she said at last. Feeling the question in his stance next to her, she struggled to find the right words. "My parents got married for love, against everyone's disapproval, because there was nothing more they wanted in the world than to spend their lives together." She paused. "This just doesn't seem right somehow."

She sighed and then tried to shake the mood off. "Want me to drive back?"

As if he knew she needed the distraction, his answer was immediate.

"Absolutely." She'd expected warnings about how to drive the precious automobile, but none came. "I could use the sleep."

In the car, pulling on her seat belt, she thought to warn him. "You know, we'll be expected for dinner with the family tomorrow night."

"Of course." He reached over and tugged on a lock of her hair. "Don't worry. They'll understand. They know why you're doing this. It's just a means to an end." Then he settled back in his seat and went to sleep.

"A means to an end. Right." She floored it. All of a sudden, she couldn't wait to get home.

When she realized that she was still thinking of *home* as her apartment, she grimaced and drove faster. She'd be spending a lot of time at the office in the coming months. Anything that kept her out of her new *home*.

Three hours later, Addy was wishing she had something to do or somewhere to go. Anything to get away from that man.

"I don't see what the big deal is." She stepped out of the car in the driveway of her great-aunt's home as Spencer cornered the front fender in three big strides and yanked the keys out of her hands. "It's not like I crashed the car. Your precious vehicle doesn't have a scratch on it."

"Hardly the point. Do you have any idea how horrifying it is to wake up in the middle of a high-speed pursuit?"

"Don't exaggerate, Reed, it doesn't suit you," she said, throwing his own words back at him. She crossed her arms and faced him in the ankle-deep snow. "I was on the shoulder by the time you woke up. And it's just a speeding ticket. Stop whining."

"Whining? Why, you—" She saw his mouth moving but no words were coming out. He spun around and walked away from her. She shrugged and bent back into the car to retrieve her backpack. If he wanted to pout about a simple speeding ticket, let him. She'd already apologized several times in the car; she was ready to let the whole thing drop.

As she stood up, her eyes took in a detail and her brain screamed a warning, but she moved too slowly. An enormous swath of snow had been scraped off the hood of the car and Spencer was nowhere to be seen on the sidewalk up to the front door.

The snowball rocketed into the back of her head right as the word *Duck!* made it to conscious thought. Too late. A shower of ice crystals exploded around her head, down the back of her neck, in her hair.

"You…bas…tard," she gasped around the sudden cold. Spinning around, she saw him standing there, grinning like a loon.

"Consider that payback for the ticket," he said and stood there, watching. Addy had grown up with three siblings. All she saw was a sitting target.

"Payback *this*."

She started sprinting for the opposite side of the BMW even before the armful of snow she swept off the roof of the car smacked him in the kisser. Scooping up more snow on the way, she prepped for her next shot.

Resisting the impulse to lower her guard and chase the snow sliding down her collar, she kept her eyes on Spencer and circled slowly around the car as he readied his throw. He threw and she ducked, letting out a triumphant shout as the missile went sailing over her head. She popped up and let loose her return fire, only to be nailed in the chest by the second snowball he'd hidden from view.

She muttered curses under her breath and got serious.

The battle raged fiercely for several minutes. Both sides took heavy losses, until Addy was sure they resembled two snowmen chasing each other around the car. After a spectacular fake out, followed by a direct hit to the enemy, she took off sprinting for the porch, hoping to make it indoors before Spencer managed to scrape the snow out of his eyes. She only managed three strides up the front walk before a slick patch of ice had her ankle twisting beneath her, spilling her to the ground in a split second.

In a moment, Spencer was crouching next to her, snowball arsenal spilling to the ground as he looked her over and dusted ice crystals off her.

"Are you okay?"

"Just glad I'm wearing gloves, or I'd be picking sidewalk out of my palms." She braced her hands beneath her to boost herself up, only to land on her butt again as a sharp pain burst in her ankle and snatched her breath. "Ouch. That's not good."

"Let me see."

He stripped off his gloves and probed at her ankle with his bare fingers, provoking a hissing intake of breath by Addy as he hit the sore spots. After a few moments, she pushed his hands away. With the thrill and energy of the snowball fight gone, she was left sitting cold and wet and sore on icy cement, feeling her body heat getting sucked out of her in rapid fashion.

"Just give me a hand up, okay?" She leveraged her good foot beneath her and started to rise. His arms were around her in an instant, pulling her up and against him in a secure grip, supporting most of her weight.

She took a tentative step and hissed again at the pain. His grip shifted.

"Wait. I'll carry you in."

"I'm fine."

"Addy, don't be foolish. You shouldn't put weight on that ankle," he began.

"Just help me walk."

"Addy."

"Look, Reed." Her tone was sharper than she'd meant it to be. She could feel her ankle throbbing now. She twisted her neck to look at him and caught the genuine concern in his eyes. She tried to gentle her voice, but embarrassment made it hard. "I appreciate the offer, but there is no way on earth I'm letting you carry me over the threshold."

All expression on his face froze and then was carefully wiped clean. She blew out a breath, then dropped her head and shook it. Even trying to be nice, she'd managed to offend him. Without a word, he hitched one arm around her and, using his free hand to support her elbow, started walking her slowly toward the house.

Once inside, Addy mumbled a few words of thanks and limped slowly up the stairs to her room. All she wanted to do right now was lie down for a while and sleep. Say, for the next six months or so. That would be the perfect nap. She could wake up like an abbreviated Rip Van Winkle to a completely new world.

On the slow walk up to the second floor, she felt his eyes on her the entire way.

At the foot of the stairs, Spencer stood with his hands in his pockets, strangling the urge he felt to bound up the stairs, scoop Addy up in his arms and then tuck her into bed.

Preferably his.

Even in pain, though—and he had seen by the whiteness in her face that she was hurting—she would rather suffer through on her own efforts than accept the barest measure of help from him.

Even on the day she'd married him.

He wasn't a fool. He knew that their marriage existed simply to allow Addy to fulfill the conditions of her great-aunt's will and that she would likely be counting the seconds until the end of the six months in order to file divorce papers.

She would *likely* do that.

Spencer had nearly made it to the altar twice before this sudden hurdle to matrimony. Each time he had proposed, it was to a woman who had seemed eminently suitable to him. Similar backgrounds, coolly professional beauties with polite relationships to their families and friends, women who seemed unflappably calm in all situations and unlikely to make overwrought emotional demands on his time.

Come to think of it, his conversations with both women regarding marriage had felt less like proposals and more like the settling of terms between two companies arranging a merger. Negotiated compromises that had pleased him at the time because they seemed to ensure that there would be no surprises down the line.

Later on, he'd come to wonder if the beginning of his unhappiness with these arrangements was that maybe, perhaps, guaranteeing no surprises turned out to be a little, well, dull. And looking ahead to a lifetime of polite relations with his own wife provoked only a yawn.

When he'd realized with each of his fiancées that he was seen as the grand prize finally won and certainly not as someone they cared about—at least not other than feeling a mild sort of gratitude for the social position marriage to Spencer Reed would provide them—breaking things off had turned out to be easy. Particularly when he spoke of his desire to have children and discovered each time that his fiancée saw children as an obstacle to enjoying her own life. They had no intention of inconveniencing themselves by being pregnant once, much less two or three times. When he'd ended it, both women had thrown mild fits of anger, as if to test his seriousness, but then after a few days had returned to their normal state of cool aplomb and moved on to the next engagement faster than he could cancel the caterers.

Spencer was left with the conviction that his existing system for determining the perfect woman for him to marry was clearly flawed in a major way.

Which was part of the reason why he'd drawn himself into this sham marriage with Addy Tyler. The other was the fact that the woman herself appealed to him on some instinctual, sexual level that had every muscle in his body tightening in need the moment she walked into a room with him.

Addy obviously did not consider being married to Spencer

Reed to be a privilege of any sort. That she'd seriously considered marrying a man who was *already* married in order to avoid the simpler solution of marrying Spencer made it abundantly clear that she didn't see his wealth or social standing as any kind of incentive.

When it came to matters of unpredictability, Addy seemed likely to represent a leap into the opposite far extreme. It didn't take much insight to see that time spent with her would always be full of surprises. And although as a rule he preferred his surprises to be limited to such matters as what vintage cabernet sauvignon would be served with dinner, he was willing to go along with it. Besides, she seemed to bring out much the same behavior in him. He was fairly sure, for instance, that he hadn't incited a snowball fight since he was twelve years old or so.

Spencer considered himself to be a fair man. Having admitted that both women he'd thought would make excellent wives had turned out to be disasters, he was willing to throw caution to the winds, in a careful sort of way, and see what sort of relationship developed between Addy and him.

Who could tell? Perhaps in six months' time they'd decide that they were getting along tolerably well, and Addy might agree that continuing on the same course would be a satisfying solution for both of them.

And if somewhere along the line he got to tug Addy, with her bright eyes, tangled hair and hunger-inspiring curves, into a private room and consummate this marriage, then the sooner the better.

Spencer had the feeling that in six months' time he wouldn't even be worrying about the private room. If he had to wait that long, on the front lawn in plain sight of the neighbors would probably suit him just fine.

That is, if he didn't throttle her first.

Heading back to the kitchen to make coffee—the solution to all problems—Spencer pictured again the look on Addy's face as she'd told him not to carry her into the house. Half embarrassed, half defiant, she'd blushed but stared him straight in the eyes.

As if he'd meant anything by the gesture other than an offer of assistance. He snorted and paced the length of the counter in front of the coffee machine. Hardly. And who would have thought Ms. Tyler put such stock in old-fashioned symbols like that? How melodramatic.

Snagging the pot as soon as it had a mug's worth of coffee in it, he poured himself a cup, ignoring the hiss of still-brewing coffee spilling onto the hot plate beneath.

Just because he was willing, maybe, to see how things developed between the two of them, didn't mean that he was going to start getting all *romantic* on her. Carrying her over the threshold. Please.

Mug in hand, Spencer started up the stairs, deciding that it was definitely time for another conversation about the rules of their relationship, although this time he'd be the one to lay down some instructions.

Don't start reading romantic gestures into simple offers of assistance being rule number one on the Reed list of How to Get Along with Your New Not-Quite Husband.

He told himself that he wasn't stomping up the stairs like an irritated, overtired child. At the entrance to Addy's room, he lifted his fist to bang soundly on the door, only stopping himself as he became aware of the complete lack of noise coming from within.

Instinct had him tempering his knock to a quiet tap on the door, which swung in an inch, not having been fully closed.

"Addy?"

There was no answer to his quiet call. Worried now—what if she'd really hurt herself or fallen and knocked herself out—Spencer debated for a split second before pushing the door open another six inches and sticking his head in for a cautious look around.

Discarded boots leaned drunkenly against each other in a spreading pool of water in the middle of the floor. That seemed to be the only concession to comfort Addy had managed to make before collapsing in exhaustion on top of her bed, fully clothed and draped diagonally over the quilt.

He called her name again, but she didn't stir. Shaking his head, Spencer backed out of the room and walked down the hall to the linen closet. He returned a minute later with an ancient and kitten-soft chenille blanket. Draping it lightly over her sleeping form, he found himself staring at her face—the little of it that was visible beneath the dark, curling hair she'd released from the ponytail and that now spilled around her in masses of ringlets. Her normal dusky gold color seemed almost whitely pale and there were lines of stress on her face, as if even in sleep she was unable to relax fully.

Moving into a new home. Getting married. Being pulled over by the police. A champion snowball fight followed by what would probably turn out to be a sprained ankle. She had in fact had quite a day.

He tucked the blanket in lightly around her shoulders then stepped to the windows and closed the curtains to dim the light in the room. At the door, he paused for a moment, wondering if there was anything else he could do for her before deciding no. His eyes on her sleeping form, he closed the door softly.

As he strode off down the hall, it occurred to him that what he'd just done could be interpreted as a romantic gesture. The thought halted him midstep for a brief moment.

"Nah." His muttered denial was less than reassuring. He shook his head and continued on his way.

He just wasn't the romantic-gesture type.

The Silhouette Reader Service™ — Here's how it works:

If offer card is missing write to: Silhouette Reader Service, 3010 Walden Ave., P.O. Box 1867, Buffalo NY 14240-1867

NO POSTAGE
NECESSARY
IF MAILED
IN THE
UNITED STATES

BUSINESS REPLY MAIL

FIRST-CLASS MAIL   PERMIT NO. 717-003   BUFFALO, NY

POSTAGE WILL BE PAID BY ADDRESSEE

SILHOUETTE READER SERVICE
3010 WALDEN AVE
PO BOX 1867
BUFFALO NY 14240-9952

GET FREE BOOKS and a FREE GIFT WHEN YOU PLAY THE...

Lucky 7

SLOT MACHINE GAME!

Just scratch off the silver box with a coin. Then check below to see the gifts you get!

YES! I have scratched off the silver box. Please send me the 2 free Silhouette Desire® books and gift for which I qualify. I understand I am under no obligation to purchase any books, as explained on the back of this card.

326 SDL D7WS   **225 SDL D7W6**

FIRST NAME   LAST NAME

ADDRESS

APT.#   CITY

STATE/PROV.   ZIP/POSTAL CODE

7 7 7	**Worth TWO FREE BOOKS plus a BONUS Mystery Gift!**
🍒 🍒 🍒	**Worth TWO FREE BOOKS!**
♣ ♣ ♣	**Worth ONE FREE BOOK!**
🔔 🔔 🔔	**TRY AGAIN!**

www.eHarlequin.com

(S-D-04/05)

Offer limited to one per household and not valid to current Silhouette Desire® subscribers. All orders subject to approval.

© 2000 HARLEQUIN ENTERPRISES LTD. ® and TM are trademarks owned by the trademark owner and/or its licensee.

DETACH AND MAIL CARD TODAY!

Six

Twenty-four hours later, Addy crawled between her sheets and back into bed, where it seemed she'd spent most of her weekend. She was cursing the name of Spencer Reed all the way.

Damn the man and his little romantic gestures.

If she weren't careful, she'd find herself starting to soften a little bit each time he did something sweet until she lost all grip of cold, hard reason and jumped on the man, preferably knocking him to the ground, where she could do with him exactly as she pleased.

She'd come very close to doing just that with him tonight, and there were still one hundred seventy-nine days to go.

When she'd woken up in a dark room the night before, it had taken her a minute to orient herself. The quiet ache of her ankle was what triggered her memory. She'd groaned aloud and fumbled at the nightstand, fairly sure that she'd seen a lamp on it the day before. The first thing that caught her eye once she'd switched on the light was the neatly rolled Ace bandage at the lamp's base.

She didn't need to be a genius to figure out who'd left that there. Which also explained the warm blanket she found herself curled up in but didn't remember crawling under when she'd lain down.

She'd been tempted to ignore the bandage but knew that she'd only hear Spencer's voice in her head, nagging her, if she had. The tenderness in her ankle as she'd wrapped the stretchy fabric in crisscross fashion around her foot and a little way up her leg had her reluctantly conceding the need to thank him for the supplies.

Limping her way downstairs and bracing her weight on railings and banisters where she could, she'd wondered how long it would be before she was able to enter a room or turn a corner in this house without wondering if she'd find Spencer waiting for her.

Probably never, she'd thought with grim humor and made a mental resolution to go out and buy a calendar so she could X off in bright red marker the days left in this odd arrangement.

In the kitchen, she'd headed for the refrigerator, hoping against hope that she might unearth some form of caffeinated cola beverage. Taped to a brand-spanking-new two-liter bottle of Diet Coke, she'd found a note covered with Spencer's now-familiar scrawl.

I'm going into the office for a while. There's plenty of ice in the freezer. Put some of it on your ankle off and on and the swelling should go down. Help yourself to anything in the kitchen. You can shop for groceries later.
S
P.S. There's herbal tea in the pantry. This was just to get your attention.

Since there'd been no one to see her, she'd let herself grin. And didn't ask why she pulled off the note and tucked it in her pocket instead of tossing it in the garbage. She'd held the precious bottle of Diet Coke in one hand as she'd hopped over to the counter and rummaged through cupboards in search of a drinking glass. Finally opening the right door, she'd immediately burst into laughter.

"I'm not kidding. Drink some tea," said the note propped up against the glasses. It went into the same pocket as its brother. Then she'd snagged herself a glass and sighed with pleasure at the hiss of escaping carbonation as she twisted the cap off the soda.

Cold beverage in one hand, bag of ice and bag of chips in the other, she'd thought about settling in for the rest of the evening with her sister's copy of *Pride and Prejudice*. A quick glance at the steep stairs back up to her room and the multiple spillable items in her hands had had her reconsidering.

Then she'd had a remarkably pleasant idea.

Fifteen minutes later, she had ensconced herself in the library with her soda and snacks within arm's reach on a small table, her foot propped up on an old embroidered footstool and a bag of ice draped over her ankle. A fire had crackled in the first throes of its attack on the new wood that had been laid in the grate, needing only the touch of a match to set it aflame. And propped on her lap, an easy find in the alphabetically organized shelves, had been an old hardcover copy of Jane Austen's novel, the pages yellowing at the edges but otherwise in perfect condition.

She'd had a lovely evening, caught up in the machinations of Elizabeth Bennet's sisters in their determination to get married, and Elizabeth's determination to save her family members from embarrassing themselves in public. Addy thought Elizabeth quite right to insist on her pride, although she knew for herself that she wouldn't have been able to remain so restrained in response to Mr. Darcy's sharp barbs or Mr. Collins's moronic ramblings. She also thought Mr. Darcy was a bit of a schmuck for his prejudice against Elizabeth's family and their lack of titled ancestry.

When she'd found herself nodding off halfway through the book and the fire burning low in the grate, she'd disposed of the empty glass and the empty bag of chips in the kitchen, dumped the melted ice down the drain and limped slowly up the stairs to bed.

She'd fallen asleep, having successfully avoided all thoughts of Spencer Reed and the uproar her marriage to him was sure to cause at the family dinner on the following evening. Waking up once during the night to the sounds of her housemate coming home, she'd glanced at her glowing alarm clock and seen that it was three in the morning. For a brief moment, she'd wondered if he was as uncomfortable now in this house as she was.

If that was the case, then she regretted the arrangement. She might occasionally want to bop him over the head with something heavy, but that didn't mean she wanted him to be unhappy. Before she started to worry about why his happiness should mean much of anything to her, Addy had reminded herself sternly that if Reed was unhappy, he might back out of their agreement and she'd lose the chance to live in this house, to own her home.

That was the only reason she worried about him. Strictly a business concern.

When she woke again, it was daylight, several hours after dawn on her first full day of being Mrs. Spencer Reed. Not that she planned on introducing herself to anyone that way, since she'd be returning to Ms. Tyler as her legal name in half a year. She managed to get herself out of bed and through a shower without too many wobbles, trying to keep quiet out of courtesy for Spencer's late night.

Only after she fumbled her way through getting a pot of coffee brewing—it seemed the least she could do—and no grumpy, sleepy man stumbled downstairs and into the kitchen in pursuit of Colombia's best, did she finally admit to herself the obvious.

Spencer had either come home only briefly the night before and then left immediately to spend the rest of the night somewhere else, or he'd gotten up very early this morning, after only a handful of hours of sleep, in order to leave the house before she awoke.

Not that either of those scenarios bothered Addy. Honestly, for all she knew, he had a girlfriend—ten of them, even— and he'd decided to sleep at her house. Or maybe he was simply trying to follow the rules she'd laid down the morning before. After all, she had requested that they try to stay out of each other's way as much as possible.

"Oh, come on," she scoffed aloud as she poured herself a mug of coffee, unwilling to abandon the entire pot to a slow death on the warmer. Besides, she didn't want him to show up later and think she'd been making coffee just for him. "I didn't mean we couldn't say hello in passing. We can be *civil* to each other."

At loose ends for the day, but convinced by each throbbing step that she was better off sticking close to home, Addy spent the day hopping cautiously around the house. She explored rooms, examined lighting and plumbing fixtures, made eyeball measures of the size of each room and felt tentative plans begin to coalesce in her mind.

By midafternoon, she was a little dusty and a little excited. And a lot irritated.

"Damn it, where is that stupid man?"

She wobbled on one foot—the other ankle too sore after the walking she'd done for her to put even the lightest pressure on it—staring up at the ceiling at the end of the hall. The knob in the center of one side of a cutout rectangle lying flush with the ceiling beckoned to her. She was positive that it led to an attic, only she couldn't reach the knob and was afraid to try and balance on a chair to get to it.

What she needed was a helpful housemate to pull the door and its accompanying ladder or stairs down so that she could get up there and take a look around.

She looked at her watch. Four o'clock in the afternoon.

Where the hell was he? They needed to leave for her mother's house in less than an hour. She glared at the trapdoor one last time and hopped back toward her room. Surely she had his cell phone number scribbled down on a piece of paper.

When the front door slammed, she pulled her head out of the cardboard box in which she'd been sure she'd stuck her files about everything Reed- and house-related. She hurried into the hall, determined to yell at him for something. As it turned out, the brief glimpse she caught of him after he bounded up the stairs and before he shut the door to his bedroom had her tongue tripping over her teeth.

Apparently at least part of his day had been spent at the gym, since he was stripping a sweaty shirt over his head as he reached the top of the stairs.

Oh, my. She'd been so focused yesterday that she'd walked right past the half-naked Spencer without a second glance. Who knew that his typical dress shirt and tie was covering up muscle like that? He rubbed the back of his neck with the T-shirt, his blond hair lying dark at the nape with sweat, and the movement of his arm as he lifted it threw the muscles of his back into sharp definition. Addy felt a purely feminine hum of pleasure start deep in her throat and knew that if there'd been another woman standing next to her, they would have turned to each other, grinned and had the same thought.

Yum.

She couldn't rip her eyes away as he hooked his thumbs into the elastic waistband of his sweatpants and started to yank them off.

The sudden clap of his bedroom door closing, cutting off the increasingly lovely sight of Spencer stripping to the buff, made her jump.

She pulled her tongue back in her mouth and shook her head sharply.

"Get a grip, girl."

So the man had a nice bod. So what? Just because it was the kind of body she liked best, not hulking, muscle-bound weight lifter but the kind of long, precisely defined muscles that spoke of a healthy friendship with sport or the gym. *Like those volleyball players on the Oak Street beach in the summer, mmm...* She shook her head again. Enough. Just be glad he didn't catch you staring at him.

But before she could turn and head back into her bedroom, his door opened. Spencer stuck his head around the edge, leading her to thoughts of what nakedness he was hiding behind it. She saw his grin as he eyed her head to toe.

"Better clean up, Mrs. Reed. We need to leave shortly if you want us to be on time for supper."

With a wink, he closed the door, and seconds later she heard the sound of the shower.

Damn. Caught after all.

Back in her room, Addy caught sight of herself in the mirror and let out a small shriek. Streaks of dust were drawn on her denim shirt and the black yoga pants she'd spent the day in. She had made it into the basement on her inspection tour, part of which was still unfinished. A cobweb was strung delicately over part of her hair and since she'd gone barefoot, her bandage was smudged with dust.

She cleaned herself up and hobbled down to the front hall before Spencer showed up, minimizing the amount of help she'd have to accept from him. He looked unfairly attractive in deep-midnight jeans and a black crewneck sweater, blond hair and blue eyes gleaming brightly in contrast to the dark clothes.

Glancing down at her own nearly identical outfit, she frowned and muttered a curse.

"What did you say?" he asked, helping her into her winter coat.

She pulled her loose hair out from under her collar, one hand braced against the little hall table. "Nothing."

He slung her scarf over her head and tied it around her neck before pulling her knit cap down until it covered her ears. She refrained from mentioning that she'd been dressing herself since she was five.

"C'mon. Give." He must have caught the look in her eye, because he simply handed her gloves over.

She tugged the Thinsulate-lined leather over her fingers and knew he wouldn't give up. "I just said we look like one of those ridiculous couples who wear I'm With Her and I'm With Him T-shirts."

His laugh rang out behind her as she turned to the door, and she felt him pat her on the head. Maybe if she pretended she was Elizabeth Bennet she could curb the instinct she felt to bite at his fingers.

"Don't worry, Addy. I promise not to rush out and buy us matching T-shirts anytime soon." His hand cupped her elbow carefully. "Let's go and face the family horde."

Afraid that if she spoke he'd hear the pain in her voice, she concentrated on trying to walk normally, but with caution, down the still-icy sidewalk.

"Salt," was all she said.

"What?"

"Salt." A quickly smothered inhale. "For the sidewalk."

"I'll take care of it tomorrow," he promised.

In the car, they were both silent. At first, Addy kept her mouth shut because she was determined not to quiz him on where he'd spent the night and the better part of the day. But soon she became absorbed in thoughts of her mother and brother and sisters. Despite the worry she felt, she was grateful to realize that she had no doubt they would support her even in such a crazy turn of events as this. At heart, she knew she could go to them with anything, no matter how serious the trouble, and they would all be there for her, ready to step solidly behind her and back her up in any way she needed.

That didn't stop her from picking incessantly at a tiny tear in her gloves in an effort to distract herself.

As they pulled to a halt on the street in front of her mother's house, she counted the cars and realized that they were the last to arrive.

"Great. Nothing like getting it all over with at once."

She didn't think Spencer had heard her. At least, not until he pressed a quick, friendly kiss to her lips as he helped her out of the car.

"Stop worrying. Everything will be fine." Her lips were still tingling from the warmth of his mouth on hers as he leaned past her into the back seat of the car. "Here. Hold these. I'll hold you."

She glanced down at the bundle he'd thrust into her arms and felt her determined coolness thaw a little bit. What must have been two or three dozen roses shone in ice-pink profusion, swathed in layers of silvery tissue. The spicy scent of expensive flowers drifted up to her nose. His voice drew her gaze to his gently smiling face.

"I'd come bearing gifts for everyone, but I don't want them to think I'm offering a bribe." He quirked an eyebrow and shrugged. "So I settled for appealing to your mother."

"Thank you for thinking of her," she said, her voice low.

When her mother met them at the door alone, Addy understood that her siblings had been instructed not to rush in, and was grateful. She handed the flowers blindly back to Spencer and stepped into her mother's embrace, was pulled close and held tight. For a few moments, she rested her head on that strong shoulder until she felt herself edging too near the boundary she'd drawn between herself and tears outside the courthouse the morning before.

She stood up straight and forced a smile. Her mother's eyes told her she was fooling no one, but Susannah smiled at her, cupped her daughter's chin in her hands and pressed a kiss to her mouth.

"All will be well, child of mine," she said and patted her on the cheek before turning to the man waiting at their side. "Spencer, my dear, welcome to the family."

"Thank you, Susannah," he answered gravely and extended the bouquet, which was ignored for the moment in favor of giving him a hug.

Addy's protest spilled out of her mouth without thought.

"He's only a part of this family for the next six months. This is just a business arrangement."

By the looks on their faces, she knew she'd insulted the one and disappointed the other. Her mother's stern voice broke in before Spencer could speak.

"Your 'arrangement'—" Addy could hear the quotation marks around the word "—with Spencer may end in six months, but we will always welcome him in our family." Her mother turned to Spencer again. "And not only because of the lengths he's gone to in order to help you."

Watching her mother link an arm through her new husband's, Addy decided that the wiser course was to shut up and follow them into the living room. After all, did she really want to protest that being married to her for the next six months would be enjoyable?

Besides, the scent of her mother's jambalaya, a family favorite, was rich in the air, and a sudden rumble in her stomach reminded her that, other than a bag of potato chips, she'd hardly eaten in the last twenty-four hours. Maybe they could get the congratulations over quickly and settle down to some nice, polite chitchat over dinner.

She'd apparently forgotten that this was her family she was talking about.

The moment they stepped into the living room, Maxie bounced up off the couch, where she'd clearly been forcibly restrained by Sarah, and rushed over to them.

"Congratulations! We've been waiting for you for simply ages," she squealed as she ran over and spun in a whirlwind of hugs and kisses from Spencer to her sister and then back again. She grabbed Spencer's arms and held them out. "God, you're such a fox. When can I come and see your guys' house?"

"The house belongs to Addy, and anytime," he answered, without at blink at the flower-strewn hat and Southern-belle dress Maxie wore. "Nice outfit, by the way."

"It's too much, I know. But it seemed like such a bridesmaidy kind of day. I mean, how often do you *have* an excuse to wear a hat with flowers on it?"

"Not often, I would imagine," he said, and kissed her on the cheek as she hugged him again.

Sarah meanwhile had come quietly up to her sister and hugged her without saying a word. Addy knew her arms were tight around her sister's thin shoulders. She whispered into Sarah's ear.

"Thank you."

"Don't worry," Sarah said quietly back, echoing their mother's words. "Everything's going to be all right."

"You'd better be right about that." She gave her sister one last squeeze and stepped back. Taller than the rest of the family, her brother stood behind Sarah, waiting his turn with grave eyes. As Sarah turned to offer her congratulations to Spencer, her brother placed his hands on Addy's shoulders, bent over and kissed her solemnly on the forehead.

"Here's to going after what you've always wanted," he said, and she knew he wasn't speaking of her hasty marriage to a man she'd known for mere weeks. Then he threw his arms around her and wrapped her in a bear hug that had her on the verge of tears again.

"If you make me cry, Christopher Robin…" she started to warn him before his big hand clapped over her mouth to shut her up and he shot a look at Spencer, who was two feet away and still talking to Sarah and Maxie.

"Jeez, sis," he muttered. "You may have brought him into the family, and Mom blessed it, but he doesn't have to be let in on everything, does he?"

"Don't worry, bro. Your secret's safe with me." She reached up a hand and ruffled his hair. He smacked it away, scowling, and put back on his stern look as he faced Spencer. Addy didn't think she'd ever loved her brother so much as when she watched him turn into "the man of the family" with her new husband.

"Reed. Thanks for marrying my sister."

"You're welcome."

The two men shook hands with the firm grasps and serious faces that showed respect for one another while withholding final judgement.

"As long as you remember that just because you're married to her doesn't entitle you to anything more. You're helping her out and we appreciate it, but that doesn't mean you automatically get to sleep with her."

Addy smacked a hand over her eyes and groaned out loud. A furious blush raced hotly over her as she listened to her brother carry his role too far. Eyes still shut, she heard Spencer's response.

"I understand. I'd have the same concerns if I were in your place. But I'm sure you know as well as I do that your sister can take care of herself."

She opened her eyes in relief at his calm answer.

"When she decides to sleep with me, it will be because she's made the choice to do so."

She didn't know whether to blind herself or gag the both of them. She yanked Spencer's arm away from where it was still held in her brother's handshake and dragged him out of the room, limping painfully.

"Will you please not encourage him to discuss my sex life in public! Or in private, for that matter! You two aren't to be discussing my sex life at all," she commanded, lowering her voice from a near shout as she realized that her family was no doubt listening to every word she said. Spencer simply grinned at her.

"You can't blame a brother for worrying about his sister," he began, until she gave him a push that backed him up against a wall. She saw his head bang into the corner of a picture frame, and hoped it stung.

"And don't think I didn't hear you. '*When* she decides to sleep with me'!" She poked him in the chest with a stiff finger. "You can get one thing through your thick head right now, mister," she began.

A swift yank had her stumbling off balance from one foot and into his arms. His hands plunged into her hair and his mouth covered hers before she had a chance to protest. And she would have. She knew it. It was just that he tasted so good and his fingers flexing against her scalp made her wish he'd tug on her hair until her head tilted back so he could run a line of kisses straight down her neck. She gave in just for a moment and dove into the kiss, her mouth opening under his, her arms shifting from pushing to pulling him closer. She was dimly aware that she'd been waiting for this kiss from the second they'd signed their marriage license.

After a minute, Spencer lifted his head, bent back for one last nipping kiss at her bottom lip and looked her straight in the eye.

"You can lay down whatever rules you like, Addy, and I'll respect them. But I've already told you—you can't pretend you don't want me. And I definitely want you."

"I can tell," she muttered and looked away. She was plastered against him like white on rice, wasn't she? She felt laughter shake him. He pulled a hand from her hair and nudged her chin back up to look at him.

"We're going to have to deal with this sooner or later."

"No, we're not." She'd argue that one until her last breath. A discreet cough from the entrance to the living room had her stepping abruptly away from him and straightening her hair. "And we're certainly not going to deal with it in my mother's hallway," she hissed.

Turning, she grinned brightly at her assembled family, who had obviously missed nothing of the entire exchange. There was more than one raised eyebrow.

"Right. Time for dinner, isn't it?"

When they answered her unspoken plea, she could have kissed them one and all.

"Right, dinner."

"Hey, I'm starving. Where's the food?"

"What are we waiting for? Let's eat."

She could even forgive her brother the dark look he shot at Spencer on his way past them to the dining room. Addy studied the floor and avoided Tyler's gaze, sure that her brother had a few things to say to her, too. If she couldn't explain her inability to stay away from Spencer to herself, she certainly wasn't going to try and offer her brother a reason for her irrational behavior.

The meal went better than she could have expected. Congratulations and friendly welcomes were offered again and toasted with a spicy red wine that held its own against her mother's Cajun meal. They broke crusty sourdough bread together and mopped up smoky-flavored sauce with the pieces as they exchanged stories.

Maxie had been cast in yet another play but was thinking of giving up her role to the understudy, since the costume designer had dropped out of school and run off to California with her skater boyfriend and Maxie had taken on that responsibility, also.

Tyler was pretty sure his manager was skimming money off the nightly drop and asked for opinions about the wisdom of telling the owner of the bar where he worked, since Tyler was the newest hire.

Sarah was researching internships but was concerned that the ones that most appealed to her were located in rural farming communities. She wasn't sure she wanted to be so far from her family and friends.

Addy's mother told a funny story about catching one of the nurses on her staff in a supply closet with one of the doctors. The tale had everyone laughing, although it made Addy wonder what they'd be saying about her lip-lock with Spencer after they left. But she was grateful that an unspoken agreement kept everyone off the topic of her new marriage.

Occasional questions were directed at Spencer. Friendly inquiries that he answered without any indication of feeling grilled by her family. Yes, construction was coming along nicely on his building, thank you. Everything should be done by summer's end, right on schedule. His parents were out of the country at the moment, but he'd e-mailed them and they were eager to meet everyone as soon as they returned, the date for which was uncertain. As the meal progressed, it became clear to Addy that her family had had more interaction with Spencer in recent days than she'd imagined. Than she herself had had, it seemed. She was embarrassed to hear him answer questions that it hadn't occurred to her to ask.

More, she was distracted by the brush of Spencer's elbow against hers and the way his thigh seemed to press against hers, even as she scooted to the far side of her chair. When he laid his hand on hers to get her attention before asking her to pass the bread, she wondered if anyone else could see the heat that flashed from his skin into hers.

"The case is going well. No, thank you, I'm driving," he said as Sarah asked with a tilt of the wine bottle if she could pour him another glass. "We should probably come to a settlement next week at the latest, which will be a relief to the Coleman family, I'm sure. They've been camping out at a relative's home ever since the mold was found in the walls of their house."

"Good," her mother said as she rose to begin clearing plates from the table. "I've been thinking about them ever since you mentioned it to me. Maxie and Christopher, will you clear the table? Sarah, we'll serve coffee in the living room. I want to take a look at your ankle, Addy. You've been limping ever since you got here."

"It's nothing," she protested as all eyes turned toward her. Damn her incessant blushing. "I slipped on some ice."

Spencer paused in the act of stacking her plate on top of his and laughed out loud. "She means to say that she slipped while sprinting for the safety of the house after I trounced her in a snowball fight."

"I was looking for cover," she lied with loud emphasis over her brother's hooted derision, "from which to continue pelting you with my superior aiming ability. You were just hoping I was going to let up on you."

"We can rematch anytime, wife of mine."

"Oh, sure, challenge the girl with the sprained ankle."

"Now it's a sprained ankle, is it?"

"Hey, maybe it'll slow me down enough to give you a fair chance."

Their eyes locked and she found herself grinning at him. She caught herself thinking that this was what she loved about him. The teasing, smart-aleck exchanges that reminded her so much of her banter with her family. Then she heard herself using the word *love* in reference to the man she'd just married for money, and slammed into the wall of confusion that seemed to surround her now. She dropped her gaze as the room emptied—her brother was giving Spencer tips on her weaknesses—and propped her head up in her hands on the dining room table.

Would it never let up? This constant roller-coaster ride from laughter to irritation to moments of weepiness. She felt as if emotions were flashing out of her skin in lightning fashion, each one barely bursting into being before another overwhelmed it. She'd always had strong feelings, embracing the passionate highs and gentling herself through the occasional lows, but she'd never felt so out of control of herself before. It was as if every time she turned around she faced another Addy in the mirror, never the same woman twice.

Her mother's hand stroked her hair with a soft touch.

"All will be well, I know," Addy said. She looked up at her mother. "If only you could tell me how to make sure."

"There is no making sure, sweetheart. There's only being kind to each other and trusting in that to get us through. Now let's take a look at that ankle."

In the living room, ankle rewrapped securely with instructions to continue the occasional icing, Addy curled up on the couch next to Sarah. She turned down Maxie's offer of coffee, not wanting to be kept up with her thoughts, and felt tiredness creep over her.

It had been quite a weekend.

She didn't realize she'd fallen asleep until someone shook her gently awake. She opened her eyes to see Spencer crouched next to her, his eyes on a level with hers where her head rested on the arm of the sofa. Her mind stumbled on the thought that the last time he'd woken her up kneeling next to her in a cozy room, he'd kissed her.

"Hey, there, sleepy one." He didn't move as she reached out a sleep-slow hand to push a stray curl off his forehead. But his eyes gleamed. "Let's get you home."

"Home. Right." She sat up and yawned. Better not to ask herself where that particular tender gesture had come from. The room was empty except for the two of them.

"They're in the kitchen, packing up leftovers," he said, answering her unasked question. "Your sisters have claimed the lot, I'm afraid."

"S'okay. Mom can always make more." Her coat and things were on the couch next to her. She let him pull her up and steady her as she wobbled on one foot and bundled herself up. Told herself that she was just folllowing her mother's instructions to be kind as she leaned on him and thanked him for helping her.

"Anytime." Surely it was okay for a husband to press a kiss to the top of his wife's head. She smiled, guessing that she must still be half-asleep to be so mellow.

Goodbyes were quick and filled with love and promises made to come visit her soon at her new residence. Her mother was the last at the door, tugging Spencer down to kiss him on the cheek and then repeating the gesture with her daughter.

"Safe home," she said.

The warmth of the car was surprising, until she realized that Spencer must have gone outside earlier to warm it up for her. She shifted her shoulders until she could watch him unobtrusively, his profile dimming and brightening in the glow of passing streetlights as they drove home. How did he manage it? She gave him little incentive to be nice to her and yet he found ways to be kind to her time after time.

At a stoplight, he turned and looked at her and smiled for a moment before the light turned green. Turning back to the road, he accelerated.

She would try to be kind, also, and trust in that.

"Thank you." The words didn't seem to be enough, so she rested her hand lightly on his arm for a moment, wondering if perhaps she could communicate her gratitude by her touch. "For being so kind to my family." Which wasn't precisely all she meant, so she forced herself to finish. "To me." She leaned her head back against the headrest, satisfied that she'd gotten it all out. Her eyes drifted shut in the quiet hiss of tires speeding through slush.

"They're easy to be kind to. I like them," she heard him say as she slipped back into the sleep she'd found in her mother's house and felt his hand reach over and take hers and squeeze gently. She meant to squeeze back but wasn't sure her tired limbs obeyed her command. And she was sure she imagined it when she heard him say, "I like you, too."

She dozed on the edge of sleep, barely awake to mumble a protest when his hand slid from hers and everything grew quiet. A moment later, the door at her side opened and she felt herself being unbuckled from the seat belt and lifted from the seat with the ease a parent would use on a sleepy toddler. She curled up and tucked her head into the warmth of his neck, knowing there was some reason she should be walking but drowsily breathing in the vanilla-and-leather scent of him as he carried her carefully to their house.

Only as she felt him mount the steps to the front door did she remember her protests of the day before. She stiffened for a moment as he fumbled with keys at the door until he hushed her.

"Shh, go back to sleep. It's not a big deal."

But it was. And she was wide awake as her husband of twenty-four hours pushed the door open and carried her over the threshold into their home.

Seven

"**Y**ou shouldn't have done that."

She squirmed out of his arms, stripping off her gloves. He let her go slowly, so that she slid the length of his body before coming to a precarious rest at his feet, his arms still encircling her. She bumped up against him as the dog bounded into them, barking happily in joy at their return and in a clear request to be let out now.

Spencer reached behind him with one hand and yanked the door open far enough for Elwood to squirm through into the cold night air. He shut the door again and pulled Addy back to him before she could escape.

"Why not?"

There were no lights on in the hall, but she could see him well enough to know he wasn't laughing at her. The cloth of his coat was cold beneath her bare hands, even as she felt his body's heat beneath.

"Because," she said, frustrated again by her lack of words in the face of the awkwardness of their relationship. Why was it that he never seemed to get tongue-tied around her? She tried to explain. "Because it's a symbol of something. Of a kind of love relationship." She stuttered to a halt. "Of something we just don't have," she finished lamely.

His hands slid down until his arms rested around her waist. She still wasn't going anywhere. In the darkness, she felt the pull of his gaze.

"I don't know what we have." His voice was low and husky and vibrated in her bones with the steady hum of a tuning fork striking just the right note. "All I know is that we're married for the next six months at least. And I for one can't get my mind off my spouse." His hands began making small circles on her lower back. "I had a hard time concentrating during dinner. All I could think of was how it felt to have my mouth on you."

Did men know that it was their words that seduced women more than anything else? Addy felt herself go under again at the spell of his.

"Me, too."

Just once, she told herself as she pulled his face down to hers. Just once she'd let herself make the first move. Then never again. But she had to have this one time, so help her, or she'd go mad.

The heat of his mouth burned into her, a warmth that raced through her body as her mouth opened and she tangled her tongue with his. Tasting him was like drinking greedily of the richest wine, a heady rush into intoxication that sent liquid fire sparking over her skin until she tangled her fingers in his hair to stop their electric tingling. But she only pulled him closer. Fiercely she attacked his mouth, taking out her frustrations in sucking bites at his lips before welcoming the thrust of his tongue against hers once more.

God, she was hot. Stifling.

"Wait." His protest as her arms left him turned to eager help as she shrugged out of her jacket and pulled her hat and scarf off to dump them on the floor. Finished, she kissed him again, their mouths connecting awkwardly as both their hands tugged at the buttons on his coat until it, too, fell to the ground in a heap at their feet. Closer now to his body, but not as close as she wanted to be, Addy let her hands roam over his shoulders and the muscles of his back that she'd eyed so hungrily only hours before, and welcomed his mouth again.

When Spencer tugged on her hair until her head tilted back, and burned the skin of her throat with hot, wet kisses, she knew what it was like to live a fantasy.

The gentle stroke of his tongue on the pulse in the hollow of her throat had her breath hitching with desire. He tugged on the handful of her sweater bunched in one fist, bending her farther backward, and she gasped as the rough fabric dragged over her hardening nipples.

That he could read her every breath showed as he bent over her arched torso and captured one aching breast with his mouth. Her hands were back in his hair, pulling him closer, pushing him away—she didn't know which, just that she was dizzy with wanting him.

When she stumbled and landed on her weak ankle, she tried to muffle her yelp, not wanting the pressure of his mouth dampening the fabric of her sweater to cease. She cursed under her breath when he stood up.

"Damn it." His words echoed hers.

He wrapped his arms around her waist, hauled her off her feet and walked her backward through the dark room until his foot struck the bottom step of the staircase. He turned, sat down heavily and pulled her across his lap. He wrapped one hand around her shoulders, fingers stroking the side of her neck, as the other raced up under her sweater, popped open the front closure of her bra, pushed it aside and cupped her bare breast.

"Now, where were we?" His whisper vibrated against the sensitive skin of her lips. She licked them to still the sensation and then licked his lips because it seemed the better idea. His tongue chased after hers. His thumb was rubbing back and forth over the pebble of her nipple while his fingernails scraped gently against the outer curve of her breast. She was moaning into his mouth as his hand shifted, his palm resting between her breasts as his fingers and thumb stretched wide until he was stroking both of her nipples at once.

Her insides melted into liquid heat. She ached between her legs with wanting him. She needed him, his clever hands and his hot mouth to be everywhere.

When his hand reached for the hem of her sweater, she was already tugging it off. Her arms were still tangled in the sleeves above her head when he bent down and sucked one nipple into his wet mouth. She arched her back, offering him more. She would offer him everything if only he wouldn't stop.

Hands free at last, she was incoherent in her demands as her hands streaked over him, pulling at his sweater, until finally she forced her hands beneath his chin, pulled his mouth off her and got his attention.

"Off." She pulled his sweater up over the smooth skin of his torso.

"Yes, ma'am." He lifted his arms and let her pull the offending garment over his head. Finally. She pressed her breasts against the hot skin of his chest and reveled in the purely sensual feel of skin on skin. The scent of him radiated and she sucked it in like pure oxygen.

Until his mouth covered hers again and she breathed him in instead. She wrapped her hands around his biceps and felt the muscles, like stone under silk, tightening beneath her fingers. Then pulled her mouth from his and attacked him with lips and tongue everywhere she could reach, lingering in places that made him groan in turn.

The strong tendons of his throat. The almost delicate ridge of his collarbone. The small, hard bump of his nipple. She dragged her fingernails down the length of his spine past the waist of his jeans and felt him shudder beneath her. He returned the favor, making her back arch with pleasure like a cat, until his long fingers were buried down the back of her jeans.

When he flexed his fingers against the bare skin of her butt, she knew he'd realized something.

"Why, Mrs. Reed," he drawled in the dark, "I do believe you aren't wearing any drawers."

"I know." She felt his grin against her mouth as she kissed him again. "Don't go thinking it's because of you. I almost always go commando."

"I'm never going to be able to look at you the same way again," he said and flexed his fingers one more time. "I'll always be thinking about getting my hands in your pants."

"Whatever. Stop talking."

Her hands framed his face as she pulled it back to hers, her tongue reaching for his as their mouths danced.

It seemed an instant and an eternity later when they paused. Spencer moved to reclaim her breast and Addy sucked in several deep breaths, flooding her system with sense-heightening oxygen. He stroked the nape of her neck with featherlight fingers and she shivered, but not from being cold. If anything, she was warmer than ever, sweating in fact, and seriously considering taking off both of their pants, when she heard Elwood bark.

She ignored the dog without a qualm and started working her hands between their two bodies, certain she could find the button fly of Spencer's jeans if she tried hard enough. Besides, the dog sounded far away.

When the barking, polite but determined, continued, Spencer lifted his head from her breast and cursed in frustration.

"Why the hell do I own a dog?" He pulled her arms off his neck and scooted her butt off his lap and onto the stair riser. "I have to let him in or he'll freeze to death. Don't move."

Five long strides carried him to the door. Elwood burst through as soon as it opened, and stopped to shake snow all over the hall and the heaps of their discarded clothing. By the time Spencer closed the door and turned back to her, Addy was on her feet, one hand braced against the wall.

The other hand she raised in front of her, palm out, to stop him where he stood.

"Aw, no, Addy. Don't do this." His request was quiet, the outline of his body dimly visible in the darkness. And the darkness made it too easy to pretend that what they'd been doing wasn't real. Was simply a fantasy come to life in a dreamland of shadow that would never come to the light of day.

She shook her head and slid her hand along the wall until she found the plate of a light switch. Turned it on.

The flood of light made her eyes blink until they adjusted, but she welcomed it. Welcomed the light and the cold air that had swept in from the outside to chill the hallway. She needed these reminders of the real world.

In the light, she saw him as he saw her. Stripped to the waist, both with jeans and boots still on. She didn't try to cover herself. The time for modesty was long past. She watched his eyes move over her nakedness and felt pleasure when their gazes locked again, knowing he wanted her even more at the sight of her.

"I want you." She saw the electricity of her words race over his body before leaping back to her own. Her knees trembled with the truth of the words and she said them again. "I want you."

The silence between them was broken only by the sounds of the dog noisily galloping off, in search of food no doubt.

"But." It wasn't even a question.

She answered it anyway.

"But I have to know what's right for me. And at the moment, that's unclear." She grimaced at the understatement of the year. "I'm not going to let myself get hurt."

"And I don't plan on hurting you."

"Plan it or not, if this goes too far, you could. Hell, you could be nothing but kind—" that word again, refrains of her mother's voice at this definitely inappropriate time "—and I could end up hurting myself. Because in six months this all comes to an end."

Her words sat between them like the uninvited guest at a party. His lips tightened. She could tell he was debating whether or not to say something, and waited for him to decide. A moment later he spoke.

"What if it doesn't?"

"Doesn't what?"

"Come to an end." He was watching her closely. She didn't know what to say, so she said nothing. When it became obvious that she wasn't going to speak, Spencer continued.

"What if in six months' time we still like each other? Get along fairly well, even. What's to stop us from letting things go from there?"

"You mean, if one of us hasn't killed the other by then, let's stay married?" She could have grinned at her phrasing—almost.

Spencer wasn't smiling. "Something like that."

"We may be legally married. And I may want the hell out of you." She reached out a hand and gripped the stairway banister. "But I am always going to want more out of marriage than that."

She turned and began making her slow way up the steps. She stopped on the third stair and looked over her shoulder at him where he stood still in front of the door. He hadn't moved an inch since she'd thrown her hand out and stopped him.

"You were right earlier," she said, trying to offer him something in the face of her withdrawal. "It's *when* I decide to go to bed with you. Not *if*."

She continued limping upward, not stopping even as she heard his voice call her name.

"Addy."

She knew he was putting something important into the shape of her name but chose to answer him lightly.

"Don't worry, you'll be the first to know when I make up my mind."

Once in her room, she headed straight for the bathroom, where she cranked on the hot water in the shower and finished peeling off her clothes. I probably ought to be taking a cold one, she thought, if only I weren't using the shower as an excuse to close one more door between myself and temptation.

Ten minutes later, hair wrapped in a towel and emotions wrapped in a firm grip of controlled reason, she stepped back into her room. The tableau that met her stopped her in her tracks.

An old-fashioned mahogany bed tray rested on the foot of her bed. On it sat a still-steaming pot of tea, a flowered tea-cup and saucer, a towel and a sealed plastic bag of ice in a metal bowl. A note card rested on top of the teacup. She picked it up.

Your mother made me promise to see that you iced that ankle again. I thought you'd rather see to it yourself. The tea is chamomile. Drink it if you have trouble falling asleep. I know I will.
S

She tucked the note into her sock drawer with its mates, re-moved the tea fixings to the safety of the nightstand and climbed into bed with the bag of ice. She draped the towel over her ankle, plopped the bag of ice on top and leaned back against a stack of pillows, determined to close her eyes and relax.

After ten minutes of staring at the opposite wall, her ankle was thoroughly chilled and her mind as thoroughly tangled in knots.

If only the man would stop being so goddamn *nice* to her, she might be able to think straight. She dropped the sloshing bag into the bowl on the floor beside the bed, turned out the light, rolled over and punched a pillow into suitable submis-sion beneath her head. She muttered the name of her husband-slash-tormentor with evil intonation and willed herself to sleep.

At some wee hour of the morning, after slugging back two cups of cool chamomile tea, she finally managed to drift off. Her dreams were filled with a darkly sardonic Mr. Darcy in the grand romantic tradition—*but he's blond and has blue eyes, her sleeping mind protested dimly*—who loomed over her and never ran out of subtly persuasive words. She felt her-self as Elizabeth struggling to fence back with a wit that seemed barely sufficient.

*"To yield readily—easily—to the persuasion of a friend is
no merit with you,"* he said to her, as if such a thing were a crime.

*"To yield without conviction is no compliment to the un-
derstanding of either,"* she answered back.

The words *Speak English, damn it!* made up the lingering
refrain in her mind when her alarm woke her from sleep to
the darkness of a winter morning at six o'clock.

She dressed in a hurry and skipped breakfast when the
smell of brewing coffee caught her in the hall.

She wasn't avoiding him. Not exactly. After all, she'd admitted that she knew they'd end up in bed together sooner or later
and explained that she needed some time to figure out how to
do that without getting too tangled up in emotions. She just
hoped that putting some space, both figurative and literal, between them might cool the fire in both their pants for a little bit.

"No yielding without conviction," she said aloud as she
opened the front door and braced herself against the icy air.

That was going to be her new motto all right. No yielding
without conviction.

As it turned out, she wasn't given the chance to be
tempted. For the next week, even when she started coming
home early or leaving late for work—not trying to run into
Spencer, of course—she didn't catch a glimpse of him. It
seemed he was as determined to give her some space as she
had been initially to have it. She gladly ignored her personal
problems at work, diving into technical problems of solving
floodplain issues and satisfying the Army Corps of Engi-
neers, who supervised such matters.

But by the time the weekend rolled around, she was feeling unjustifiably neglected and starting to get irritated again.

When Saturday morning dawned bright and unseasonably
warm after a week of gloomy weather, she decided to take a
page from Spencer's book. She left a note propped against a
brewing pot of coffee, snagged a couple of the dozen rubber
doggy balls rolling around the house, hooked a leash on Elwood and headed out.

* * *

He found her a half hour later in the park down the street.

The coffee had lured him out of bed, and when the caffeine had finally woken him up to coherent thought, he'd read her note. He'd hoped that avoiding Addy for a few days would draw her back into conversation with him. Smiling, he'd folded the card in one hand, wrapped the other around his mug and headed back upstairs to dress.

At the park, his approach went unobserved. Addy was laughing out loud as she watched Elwood tumble head over heels in a vain effort to brake himself as he overtook the red rubber ball she'd pitched for him. Both the dog and the woman were filthy, evidence of multiple spills in the muddy, melting snow, but it was clear that neither of them cared a bit. When Addy stuck two fingers in her mouth and whistled, Elwood raced back to her, ball clenched in his drooling mouth, and then danced away as she tried to grab it from him.

"Elwood, come here! Here! You silly dog!" she shouted at him. She chased him for a few steps and then stopped. "Come! I can't throw it for you if you won't give it back." The dog slinked toward her, teasing in his offer to hand over the ball, and then leapt away again as she stooped for it. Then he spotted Spencer and galloped over to him, barking around a mouthful of ball all the way.

Elwood skidded to a halt at his feet and promptly dropped the ball. Spencer bent over and ruffled the dog's wet fur, thumping him lightly on the sides a couple times in praise.

"Good dog."

"Traitor." She was grinning at him as she jogged over, even as she stuck her tongue out at the dog. "I've chased him for a good half mile every time before he lets me throw the ball."

Her cheeks and nose were red from the cold, and dark curls rioted from under the edge of her knit cap. Her eyes squinted until she shaded them from the glare of sunlight reflecting off snow, and when she knelt down in the muck and hugged his goofy, drooling dog, Spencer didn't think she had ever looked sexier.

"Down, boy." The words were directed as much to himself as to the dog when Elwood jumped up and planted two wet paws on his chest.

"Gorgeous day, isn't it?"

"Absolutely." He couldn't take his eyes off her.

"Your throw." She glanced down at the ball resting next to his boot.

He scooped it up and tossed it to her, the dog's tail thumping him in the legs in anticipation of another run.

"Be my guest."

She whipped it high and long with a pitcher's arm that told him she'd spent hours on a baseball field as a kid.

"Nice arm." She cocked her head at him, still grinning. He decided she could do with a little teasing. "At least you don't throw like a girl."

"Little League All-Star Pitcher, three years running," she said and took off sprinting after the dog. And just like that, they were back to being friends again. If he occasionally caught her eyeing him the way she'd gauge a scale in the produce department of a supermarket, trying to figure out if she had bagged too much or not enough, he ignored it and threw the ball for Elwood again.

Back at the house, they ate lunch together, devouring sandwiches while standing in the kitchen, too hungry to head for a table. Then they separated to their own pursuits, Addy to work on the detailed plan of the house she'd begun drawing up in her spare time and Spencer to the never-ending review of documents that flowed over his desk. But not before they both casually mentioned that they'd probably be hungry for dinner around seven.

Dinner was a pizza delivered with a Mason-Dixon Line split of toppings, all the meats on one side, all the veggies on the other. Addy dug into her sausage-, pepperoni- and ham-encrusted pizza, eyeing his green peppers, olives, tomatoes and mushrooms dubiously. *The Maltese Falcon* was playing on the public television station.

"Whatever floats your boat," she said and settled into her corner of the couch with a napkin in her lap.

The next morning, they took Elwood for a long walk along the frozen lakeshore and chatted amiably about their upcoming weeks. When Maxie showed up that afternoon, Sarah in tow and protesting loudly about the interruption of her study time, Spencer said hello and then ducked into the office off his bedroom, leaving the women to themselves as Addy showed them around the house. The sound of their laughter and conversation sometimes reached him through the walls and he surprised himself by finding the noise charming rather than disruptive.

A tap on his door signaled a polite interruption.

"Sorry to bother," Addy said as she stuck her head in the room. "Do we have a step stool?"

"No bother. What for?"

She grinned and ducked her head a little.

"I showed my sisters the trapdoor to the attic and we're all dying to see what's up there." She shrugged and looked sheepish. "I think Maxie hopes we'll find some kind of long-lost treasure."

He leaned back from his desk and stretched hugely. "Come on, 'fess up," he said through a sudden, jaw-cracking yawn. "You're hoping for it, too."

She pursed her lips, then gave it up and shrugged, laughing. "You never know what you'll find unless you look."

"Indeed."

He scraped her head to toe with one scorching glance and had the pleasure of watching her blush.

"Back of the pantry door. It's hanging, folded up."

Her quick escape from the room left him grinning as he turned back to the drily written documents on his desk. Five minutes later, when the chatter from the hall transformed into shrieks and shouts leaking through the ceiling above his head, Spencer gave up pretending that he didn't want to join them in their discoveries and went in search of the three sisters.

The rickety wooden ladder that hung unfolded from the open trapdoor looked ancient in design and dust, but seemed sturdy enough when he shook it on its hinges. He knew the sisters had made it successfully up, could hear them dragging around what sounded like enormous pieces of furniture, but he was twice the size of any one of them. Hoping he wasn't going to end up breaking his neck, he set one foot on the first tread and started to climb.

Poking his head into the attic at last, he sneezed immediately. Great buffalo clouds of dust were roaming, awakened by the zeal with which Maxie, Sarah and Addy rummaged in a metropolis of stacked boxes and trunks.

Looking up from where she knelt over a box of purely awful nylon cardigans from the fifties, Addy caught sight of Spencer eyeing them.

Like an orderly at a mental hospital, debating whether it was safe to approach a bunch of inmates gone on a rampage, she thought, and called out to him.

"It's safe, I promise. Just don't stand still and drape a sheet over yourself or Maxie may attack."

"Hey!" Her baby sister popped up from behind a drunken pile of small, round boxes. Perched on her short, dusty curls, a Jackie O. pillbox hat complete with veil tilted precariously on top of an emerald-green silk turban. "If he's not a hatbox, he's safe."

Spencer finished his climb into the attic and made his way through the maze to where Addy knelt.

"And the carnage begins."

"Yup. God, look at these, they're awful." She held up a sweater that felt like knitted Teflon and had enormous yellow flowers appliquéd over a burnt orange background. "Indestructible, I bet. This cardigan will still be around when humans have vanished from the face of the earth. Unfortunately."

He knelt down next to her, ran a hand over the next sweater in the box and grimaced at the texture. "Found any buried treasure yet?"

"Not exactly." She smiled at him and then sneezed. He followed suit two seconds later. Dust swirled. "Maxie's in rapture over the hats, but most of the rest seems to be decades of canceled checks and receipts. Interesting to a sociologist, I'm sure, but not so much for us ordinary humans hoping for nineteenth-century ball gowns or ribbon-tied bundles of old love letters."

"Too bad."

She started to stand up, accepted his helping hand to pull her upright, even though her ankle wasn't bothering her these days. "Well, I don't think Great-Aunt Adeline was much of the love-letter type."

"Are you?"

"What?"

"The love-letter type?" Her hand still rested in his. He hadn't let go, and she couldn't seem to find the urge to pull away, even though she knew she was smudging him with grit and dirt.

"I don't know. No one's ever written me a love letter before. At least, not since sixth grade." Her sisters were only ten feet away, but it felt as if she were alone in the dimly lit, slope-ceilinged room with him. She thought of the small stack of note cards hidden away in her sock drawer, then shrugged. "I like to think I would be."

"Interesting." His thumb was rubbing over the ridge of her knuckles, until he suddenly dropped her hand and walked away. Stopping at the top of the ladder in the floor, he called out, "Lunchtime, ladies. Any requests for sandwiches from the deli?"

As her sisters shouted out their orders and thanks, Addy stood there squinting with narrowed eyes at Spencer, who ignored her.

Interesting?

The man starts a conversation about love letters, decides it's *interesting* that she might be the love-letter type and then just walks coolly away and thinks about lunch?

He was definitely trying to drive her insane.

Sarah popped out from behind a hidden branch of the maze, lugging a six-foot-tall tarnished silver birdcage on a stand behind her.

"Look at this! Isn't the wirework beautiful?"

"Beautiful." Addy's voice was steamroller flat. When Sarah cocked her head to one side and gave her a quizzical look, she shook off her immobility and stepped over the box at her feet to her sister. She put some life back in her words. "Really, it's gorgeous. Why don't we try to bring it downstairs and see if we can clean it up?"

Putting all thought of love letters from her mind, she spent the rest of the afternoon enjoying her sisters' company, pulling Sarah aside to tell her how much she was enjoying *Pride and Prejudice* and getting her next recommendation at the same time. When the light began fading from the sky, they hit the showers, a sister in each guest room. Being much the same size, Sarah and Maxie raided Addy's closet for clean clothes to wear to their mother's for dinner.

Spencer joined them, of course, and the weekend ended quietly with him following Addy up to the second floor, back at home, and heading right past her to his bedroom. He turned at the door for a minute, smiled at her where she stood at the top of the stairs and said good-night.

The door closed behind him and she wondered why she felt as if she was missing something. She went to bed and had troubled dreams of incompleteness and Elizabeth Bennet looking for a vanished Mr. Darcy, whose pride she had wounded through an insistence on her own misguided perception of him.

Swearing off nineteenth-century romance novels when she woke in the morning, she began her day determined to be thankful for this newfound sense of friendship with Spencer and leave it at that. And indeed her days fell into an easy pattern of long hours at the office, with the occasional shared evening meal with Spencer at home. Some days, their busy schedules meant they didn't see each other, but they both continued in the unspoken but now comfortable habit of leaving each other little notes. He asked her if she could let the dog out when he knew he'd be staying late at the office. She offered him a choice of blow-'em-up action or slapstick comedy when she decided to rent a movie for the evening.

And through it all, even through late-night movie marathons that ended with them both asleep on the couch until one woke the other and they stumbled off to bed, Spencer never made a move in her direction. The hum of sexual tension could still be felt far below the surface, but she might as well have been his best buddy for all he showed his awareness of it.

Addy told herself to be glad. He was only doing what she'd asked of him and it was probably for the best that she didn't get more tangled up with this man who would be gone by summer's end.

Then she called herself a fool for not believing a word of her own lecture.

The weather continued unseasonably warm for Chicago as the weeks passed, spring deciding to skip the usual late-April blizzards that reminded Chicagoans not to break out their shorts and tank tops until after Memorial Day. After the second or third sunny, if chilly, weekend in a row with no snow on the ground, Addy decided to take a chance and plant some summer bulbs in the garden at the base of the front porch.

She raided a nursery of their stock of daylily and dahlia bulbs on the way home from work on a Friday. The spring light hung softly in the sky that evening as she ruled lines representing the garden on graph paper and orchestrated the placement of each bulb in the thawing ground. When she threw her pencil down at midnight, she crumpled the paper in her fist and admitted that she was only distracting herself from listening for Spencer to come home. She finally fell asleep, still listening for him.

In the morning, determined not to spend the day as she had the evening, mooning over him, she lazed in bed until ten, reaching the final chapters of *Pride and Prejudice.* She'd been unable to uphold her vow to give it up and stopped now, a handful of pages from the end, because she didn't want the story to come to a halt.

Finally bouncing out of bed, certain she'd heard Spencer leaving with Elwood earlier, she headed down to her garden, making a brief pit stop in the kitchen to snag a couple of granola bars and stuff them in her pocket. Outside, the ground proved to be harder than she'd expected, so she went in search of a shovel. There was a disreputable-looking shed at the back of the property that seemed likely to contain gardening tools.

Rounding the corner of the house, she skidded and cartwheeled her arms as she slipped on the edges of what looked like a lake of mud and water.

Parked in the middle of this new geological feature was an enormous blue plastic tub, in which sat a happily soapy Elwood, a crown of bubbles slipping off the back of his wet head as he barked at the sight of her. Spencer's back was to her, presenting her with the fine prospect of his naked torso, bare to the waist. She spied his sweatshirt draped like a flag over a nearby bush. He'd caught some sun during what was obviously bath time, and the faint flush of color only added polish to the muscles sliding under bare skin.

Stop drooling, girl. It's nothing you ain't seen before.

That she'd been wondering for the past several weeks if she'd see it again made the "stop drooling" command difficult to follow. She swallowed hard before she spoke.

"Bath time?"

Spencer shaded his eyes when he turned, a hose in one hand dripping water.

"Wanna join in?"

"No, thanks." It was a beautiful day for late April, but it wasn't *that* warm. She glanced back at Spencer's face and caught the instant that a very bad idea took shape in his mind. "Don't you dare."

"Dare what?" His fist tightened for a second on the nozzle and a jet of icy cold water blasted the soggy earth at her feet. "Oops. Must've slipped."

"Reed, I swear to you—" And she took off shrieking as he aimed the nozzle at her butt and soaked her pants. Passing the tub, she scooped a softball-size sponge out of the water and nailed him in the chest with it, but she had no more ammo and he had the hose. Thirty seconds later, she was drenched, clothes plastered to her skin, facing him with murder in her eye.

He walked up to her, ran a finger down her nose and flicked water droplets off it. Dropped his gaze to her chest.

"I've never had my own private wet T-shirt contest before." She was immediately aware of her breasts, wet cotton molded around nipples hard with the cold, and shivered, anticipation overriding the chill.

He knelt at her feet as the dog trotted over to say hello, and looked up at her, squinting in the sun.

"You'd better go inside and change. Wouldn't want you to catch cold." Rising, he strolled back to the tub.

Her jaw dropped.

She waited until she was inside the house to let out a shriek of raging frustration.

"Do I have to hit him over the head with a two-by-four?" Her shout echoed in the empty house.

When she took matters into her own hands, she decided no one could blame her. A woman could only be pushed so far before she needed to jump a man's bones just to get thoughts of him naked out of her head.

The click of the catch releasing beneath Addy's hand as she turned the knob to Spencer's bedroom was loud in the quiet house at midnight. Holding her breath, suddenly nervous now that she was actually going through with it, she eased the door open and slid through, closing it softly behind her. Moonlight glowing through the window picked out the straight edges of furniture. The long, low line of a bureau. A high, spindle-backed chair. The straight columns of his canopyless four-poster bed.

The curved lines of Spencer's form facedown on the bed, a sheet slung low over his hips, one arm buried beneath a pillow, the other flung out at his side.

She stepped to the side of the bed and watched him. The rise and fall of his breath was visible, slow and even. His face, softer in sleep, looked gentle. She shifted her weight from one foot to the other. With a soft expulsion of breath, she dropped her shoulders. Glanced at the bedside clock. 12:05 a.m.

She couldn't do this. She turned to leave.

And found herself halted by the sudden shackle of a hand gripping her wrist.

"Where you going?"

His voice sounded sleepy but his eyes were wide open and resting on her as she stood between the bed and the window, backlit by the moonlight. She was conscious of every inch of her bare skin exposed in the skimpy tank top and cotton boxers she wore. She couldn't think of a thing to say.

"Just stopping in to say hi?"

She heard in his voice the willingness to let her walk out of the room if she said yes. And suddenly it was very easy, simple even, to find the right words.

"As you pointed out to me once before, Mr. Reed," she said and stepped closer to the bed. "We are married."

Eight

When she yielded, she yielded with conviction.

The slightest tug on her hand had Addy tumbling into his bed. Spencer rolled over as she fell forward so that she landed on top of him, breasts flattened against his bare chest, elbows planted on either side of his head.

His head framed between her forearms, she leaned above him and watched her shadow dim the silver edging of moonlight on his features. She lowered her head and traced the lines from memory with her mouth, skimming her lips over the edge of his jaw, the arch of his brow. Ran the tip of her tongue lightly over the outline of his lips, until his open mouth surged up to capture hers. His arms, loose around her waist, tightened almost painfully as he hugged her to him and rolled over until she lay beneath him.

She spread her legs wider as he settled between them, and shifted her hips until the hardness of him settled on just the right spot.

"God." The words came between swooping attacks on her

face and neck with his open mouth. "I thought you were never going to get here."

"I wasn't sure you still wanted me to show up."

Her hands were urgent in their need to feel the heat of him, sculpting the curves and planes of his hard back down to a narrow waist and hips. Reaching farther, she found nothing but skin.

The man slept naked. Praise be. It saved time.

"Not sure?"

He reached down and braceleted her wrists with his hands. Dragged them up over her head until she was forced to lie still and pay attention to what he was saying. Unbelievably, he was laughing.

She could feel his body shaking against some very sensitive areas.

"Addy. Sweetheart." His teeth were a pale flash above her as he smiled. "I'll probably have a five-hundred-dollar water bill next month from all the cold showers I've been taking."

"You have been awfully clean lately," she said and licked her lips, tugging to free her hands. Spencer braced himself above her on one arm, the other still clasping both of her wrists. All she could think of was that he wasn't kissing her.

She twisted a little in his grasp, wanting her hands on him again, but he didn't let go. She could see him, his eyes on her as her back arched and her breasts pushed up at him, taut nipples visibly peaking against the thin cotton.

She watched him watching her. Knew pleasure at the sight of her own breasts moving toward him on a deep inhale and felt heat bloom between her legs. She wrapped her thighs around his hips and locked her heels behind his back, searching for more pressure and clenching her muscles tightly around him.

He let go of her wrists for an instant, fisting his hand in the hem of her loose tank top and yanking it with one pull up over her head, tangling her too-slow hands in fabric cuffs.

"You can still stop this, even now." His lake-blue eyes were dark above her, his golden hair bleached pale in the moonlight. He rested his palm on her stomach, his hand spread possessively over her rib cage, the tips of his fingers brushing the undersides of her breasts. "Tell me this isn't right for you and I'll stop. But I'm warning you," he murmured, dipping his head and running the tip of his tongue along her collarbone and then in a straight line down the slope of her breast, stopping a hair's breadth from her nipple. His warm breath feathered over her skin. She pressed her shoulders into the mattress to make him take her in his mouth. "I'll probably jump out the window if you do."

He pulled her nipple into his mouth and curled his tongue around her, sucking lightly. Covered her other breast with his palm, tracing lacelike patterns on her shivering skin. The combined sensations burst in her like sudden white heat after a long, sizzling fuse.

She settled her linked hands behind his neck and pressed him to the heart of her. Freeing herself, she tossed her tank top into the dark room and yanked hard on his hair.

"Ouch. Stop it. Busy here." He barely lifted his head.

Soft hair waved between her fingers and what felt like the heat of the sun was radiating from his mouth to every cell in her body. But she wanted more. Now.

She yanked again and dragged his face up to hers. Nose to nose in the dark, she made her intentions clear.

"It's right for me." She gentled her hands on him, stroking her fingers through the hair she'd abused so roughly. "I want you. Inside me." She could feel her own wet, melting heat and knew she was ready. "Now."

"Just one more thing," he said, and slid down her body, hooking his thumbs in the waistband of her pajama shorts and dragging them down her legs.

"Excellent idea." She barely got the words out before he slid his palms from her ankles up the length of her legs, pushing her thighs apart, and the heat of his mouth on her had her gasping for air.

"Reed." His name rode on a low moan pushed out from deep inside her.

"You only call me that when you're impatient," he said, and his breath on the most sensitive part of her was pure torture. His thumbs traced lines of fire up and down the inner crease of her thighs. "Just let me do this. I've been imagining it forever."

His low hum of approval was still vibrating on his lips as he bent back to her, and the touch made her cry out. Clenching spasms wracked her body until she couldn't even feel him touching because she was tight, so tightly spinning, and then melting in sudden release.

The last cry was still on her lips as he moved up her body and eased himself inside her in one smooth motion. The absolute rightness of the feeling, of their two bodies joined in exquisite stillness, made her hand tremble as she lifted it to his face. She stroked his cheek. And then he began to move and she was lost again to pure sensation, his flesh on hers, inside and out.

She barely heard herself whimper as she climaxed. He surged against her one last time and she felt him collapse over her. They were both heaving deep breaths and her muscles were weak and achy. She was warm where he lay on her, but the sheen of sweat on her limbs began to chill. With one tired arm, she reached down, dragged a sheet up over the both of them and fell asleep with Spencer still inside her.

When Addy woke up, the room was still dark. Spencer lay facedown next to her, one arm draped over her waist, his face buried in a pillow. She levered herself up on one elbow and peered over his sleeping form at the digital clock.

Less than three hours had passed since she'd walked into his room. Three hours and a world of difference.

She looked at her lover, *her husband,* laying next to her and wished she could see his face. Suddenly it seemed to her that he was a stranger. A stranger she was sleeping with, was married to. It was silly, but with only his back visible to her, it worried her that she might not be able to pick him out of a lineup. She tried to grin at the idea, a row of men all stripped to the waist and her behind a two-way mirror, lips pursed, saying, "I'm not sure…could you ask number three to flex?" But the kernel of truth in the idea killed the humor.

Before she could change her mind, before she could lean over and press her mouth to his shoulder and stroke his hair until he awoke, she swung her legs over the edge of the bed, eased his arm off her lap and stood up. She stopped on her way to the door to scoop up her tank top, guessed that her shorts were kicked to the bottom of his bed, under the sheet, and decided to leave them behind.

She eased the door open and left as quietly as she'd entered. Back in her room, the sheets were cold and her body was sore as she crawled into her own bed. She set the alarm and curled up in a tight ball in the center of the bed. Sleep was a long time coming.

In the morning, she felt awkward, wondering if by leaving in the middle of the night she'd made things worse between them than if she'd stayed. She knew she'd been right, but still, regret washed her certainty away.

Suppose she had stayed. She didn't know what would have been more difficult: to wake up to distance, Spencer gone from the bed before her or emotionally absent, or to wake up to moments of tenderness and gentle touch, like a husband and wife in love and coming to consciousness in each other's arms, with a long slow morning of making love beckoning.

But it was Monday morning and the real world waited. They were husband and wife, but they weren't in love.

And if she let herself live a fantasy when she was making love with him, she had to step out of that fantasy once the love-making stopped.

She lingered in the kitchen, eyeing her watch but unwilling to leave the house without seeing Spencer. When she heard his heavy footsteps on the stairs, she turned to the counter and poured him a mug of coffee, needing something to do so that she wasn't just standing there, waiting for him.

She stepped back from the counter when he entered the room, leaving the full mug and indicating with her chin that it was for him, knowing by now that he wasn't capable of speech for a minute.

He splashed cream in the mug and then drained it in long swallows. Poured himself another cup and sipped it like a normal human being, eyes opening as the heat jump-started his system even before the caffeine hit him. He looked at her and made a wordless up-and-down gesture at her body with one hand. She read the question with ease.

"I have a zoning meeting tonight in Evanston." Glancing down at herself, she wondered if it was the first time he'd seen her out of jeans. She imagined that the women he normally dated wore outfits like this all the time. The little black suit had cost her a month's pay but went over well with aldermen and city council members when she had to make presentations.

Eyeing him, she conceded that he certainly didn't need a suit to look good. The black sweatpants he wore rode low enough that she could see the wedge of muscle defining his hip bone. She remembered putting her mouth there the night before.

She dragged her eyes back up to his face as he leaned that hip against the counter and crossed his ankles. He cradled the coffee mug in both hands. The power of speech had returned to him.

"I didn't think you'd leave."

His voice was calm, measured. She envied him his cool, unemotional mind-set as she struggled to find a way to explain why she had.

"I had to," she began. When he just waited for her, she remembered something he'd said to her last night. "Coming to you last night was right for me. For us, I hope. But staying until morning wouldn't have been." She knew that was no explanation but hoped it would be enough for him.

"Can you tell me why?"

Apparently not. Damn. More words.

"Look. If we were dating—" he lifted an eyebrow at her words "—sleeping together, whatever you call it, things would follow a certain course." She started pacing, needing the outlet for her energy. The unfamiliar sounding of her heels clicking on the slate-tiled floor followed her. "Some days we'd see each other, some days we wouldn't, right?" He nodded slowly, as if waiting to see where she would take this. "Maybe you'd stay over at my place one night and maybe I'd stay over at yours the next."

His interruption was quick and to the point. "And I'd want you to stay until the morning every time."

Clearly she'd chosen the wrong analogy.

She stopped walking and faced him with all she had left. The truth.

"You may have carried me over the threshold, Spencer, but I'm not ready to start acting like your wife, sharing a bed and a bathroom every day, just because I slept with you."

She was holding her breath as she waited for him to say something. When he put the coffee mug down and walked over to her, Addy didn't know whether to step back or move toward him. Indecision rooted her on the spot.

Stopping in front of her, Spencer reached out, cradled her face in his hands and kissed her on the mouth. His lips were gentle on hers for a moment. Then he lifted his head and looked in her eyes.

"Okay."

She could breathe again. Her inhale was shaky as she leaned into him, wrapping her arms around him, hoping he could feel the gratitude in her hug. Once again, he was letting her set the rules.

And if she wondered for a moment why he never seemed to want more than she offered, that was her own damn fault.

Pulling away, he swatted her on the butt and sent her out the door.

"Go, I know you're late." She shot a last look of thanks over her shoulder as she scooped the briefcase she'd exchanged for her usual backpack off the floor and left. He winked at her. "Feel free to stop in and say hi when you get home."

She knew she shouldn't. She'd managed to get through an entire conversation about how she didn't want to be with him every night without ruining everything. The smart thing to do would be to hold back, sleep alone and give an example of what she meant. But the house was so quiet when Addy finally got home and her room was so empty. During the entire day, thoughts of him had never been far from her mind.

So she forgave herself when she went back to Spencer's room, not trying to sneak in without waking him this time. He woke in a moment and reached for her in the dark. She flowed over him, already naked as he was, and covered his mouth with her own, not wanting the risk of words.

Their loving was silent except for the soft cries of pleasure she couldn't keep from spilling past her lips. She curved over him in the night until he shuddered beneath her, and then found her own climax riding on the wave of his.

When he wrapped an arm around her as she lay next to him, sweat cooling on her skin, she let him. But she didn't close her eyes, and when she knew that he slept, she left him and went back to her room.

She took the next day off work, thinking she needed the time at home alone to clear her mind. But after an hour of sitting with her thoughts and a cup of tea, on an armchair near a sunny window, she decided that her thoughts were beyond help and got up again.

Spencer found her on her knees in one of the upstairs bathrooms, peeling the last remnants of a puce-green wallpaper from the edge of the floorboards. When she looked up, she saw that he was holding a bottle of Diet Coke and a wax-paper-wrapped sandwich out to her.

"Somehow I knew you'd be home early today."

"Didn't go in at all. Personal day." A stray curl had escaped from the casual braid she'd pulled her hair back in. She brushed it off her forehead with the back of one hand, reached out with the other. He knew her priorities and handed her the cola first. She twisted the lid off and drank as he eyed the walls, then her messy clothes. She shrugged.

"I know. It's not technically my house yet. But no one should have to live with a color like that."

He smiled at her. "You're absolutely right."

Cans of paint were lined up on the floor like soldiers. He leaned over and looked at the sample splotches of paint on each lid, all shades of blue.

"I thought it should look like the ocean in here," she said.

"Give me a minute to change and I'll help you sand it down."

She'd been enjoying doing the work herself but found that she welcomed the idea of working with Spencer, too. When he came back to the bathroom in old jeans and a T-shirt, she handed him a white face mask, stretched the elastic band of her mask over her hair and set about raising some dust.

Not until they took a break and headed down to the kitchen, careful not to touch anything with their plaster-powder–covered hands, did she find out that he'd had a reason for searching her out so early in the afternoon.

After minimal cleanup—what her mother would call *a lick and a polish*—they grabbed drinks and stepped out the back door to get some fresh air. Addy stood halfway down the stairs while Spencer walked down to the grass.

"Thanks for the help," she said, sucking clean, crisp air deep into her lungs. "I'm glad you came home early."

"Well, I wanted to talk to you."

She refused to tense up at the thought of another uncomfortable conversation.

"We haven't exactly been careful, Addy."

She gave him a blank look, and reached a hand up to feel for the face mask still perched on top of her curls, sure she had made them both follow such a basic safety precaution.

Spencer rolled his eyes at her.

"I'm talking about safety in the bedroom, not the bath."

Comprehension dawned. She sat down hard on the cement

step. Their two nights together rushed through her mind in vivid detail, right down to the sensation of having him inside her.

Bare skin on bare skin.

She didn't say anything, staring at her hands as they strangled the neck of the cola bottle and trying to figure out how she'd lost her mind so completely that she'd let this happen.

"Are you on anything?" His question lifted her head. She laughed harshly.

"Other than the occasional aspirin?" She shook her head. "No. It's been so long—Jesus, how could I be so stupid? The last thing I need is to end up an—"

"Unwed mother?" He finished her sentence. The silence between them was its own comment.

"It'd end up being exactly that," she said finally. When he opened his mouth to speak, she kept talking. She didn't want to hear his denial or his promises. "Look, let's not go jumping to any conclusions here." She did a rapid mental count of days. "I'm probably fine. And if I have a problem, that's what it is. My problem."

He came over to the steps and stood between her bent knees. Taking the bottle from her, he set it on the stairs and gathered her hands in his.

"Don't be ridiculous. If *we* have a problem, it's ours, and I want you to tell me immediately." She set her lips together and eventually nodded. She could agree with his intentions without promising anything. "As far as the rest goes, I've taken care of it."

Statistics about the failure rate of condoms flashed to the front of her mind. "That's fine, but twice as safe is better. I'll call my doctor tomorrow."

But when she spoke to her doctor the next morning, the woman told her that she'd need to wait until they were sure she wasn't pregnant. She could start the Pill on her next cycle, though.

Stress at the idea of an unwanted pregnancy cooled things between them for a little while but not during the night. Addy didn't think anything could keep her from Spencer's bed in the middle of the night, from the shivering pleasure she found there time after time. But it was harder to look at him in the middle of the afternoon and not wonder if she was making such a mess of her life that she might never be able to repair it.

Try as she might, she couldn't make herself care about that.

Another weekend rolled around and she'd settled into a state of assumed calm, when Spencer pitched another curveball at her.

"You want me to what?"

Her bottle of cola rattled as she slammed it down on the little round-topped wrought-iron table. The weather was warm enough on the first day of May that they'd decided to grill dinner outside and eat in the backyard. It had been a very pleasant meal up until right about now.

Spencer was grinning at her from across the table, the Chinese paper lanterns she'd strung up over the back door making his hair shine red-gold. The smell of hickory smoke and steak, grilled to perfection, still hung in the air.

"It's not like I'm daring you to strip naked and run around the block."

"I did that in college," she retorted. "Won fifty bucks on a bet and enjoyed it a lot more than what you're proposing."

He laughed out loud. "Trust me. This is much easier."

"Says you."

"It's just dinner with a colleague and his wife." He snagged her free hand and pressed a quick kiss to her knuckles. She wasn't falling for that. "C'mon. Come with me. You can tell 'em you're my girlfriend," he offered in persuasion.

She stuck her tongue out at him. "I don't know if that's better or worse than the truth."

"Fine. You can tell them you're my willing sex slave."

"Well, that much is true," she said, frowning, until his sudden hot look and the hand he slid up her arm to stroke at the crook of her elbow reminded her that she wasn't to be persuaded. "Besides, it's not just dinner. It's dinner and the symphony." She said the last word as if she was scraping something icky off her tongue.

"It's the symphony and then a late dinner. And you'll like it, I promise you."

"You may have only known me for a couple of months, Reed, but even that short of a time ought to have made it clear to you that I am not exactly the symphony kind of girl." She pulled her hand free and grabbed her drink, taking a healthy swig. "Put me in a blues bar or a jazz club and I'm right at home." She smiled at the thought. "Hell, and there's nothing better than getting hot and sweaty dancing in a jam-packed reggae bar until dawn."

"I can think of a better way to get hot and sweaty, and you could even call it dancing." The devil danced in his eyes as he ran a bare foot up her leg until his toes wriggled in her lap. She swatted at him.

"Stop distracting me. My point is that I'm not a pearls-and-cocktail-dress–wearing, fluty-music–liking woman."

"You pulled a suit out of that disaster you call a closet. I'm sure you've got a dress stuffed in there somewhere."

"That's not the issue."

"Fine." He settled back in his chair, all limbs back where they belonged. She nodded decisively, glad she'd made her point. "I dare you."

She gritted her teeth, willing her mouth shut. It was a no-win contest. She gave up in a huff. "My brother talks too much," she muttered. "One of these days I'm going to tell you his real name, and we'll see how he likes it then."

"Why, Addy, whatever do you mean?"

She eyed her bottle and wondered if the two inches of cola left in the bottom would spray far enough to wipe the grin off Spencer's face if she shook it up enough.

"Only Tyler knows just how powerless I am to resist a dare." She'd plot her sibling's revenge later, and it would be painful. She was losing this round, but she wanted something in return. "Fine. The symphony and dinner. But then you have to come with me on an outing of my choosing."

"Done." She could see that he wasn't worried.

"A Cubs game. Wrigley Field. Bleacher seats."

"No problem."

"A day game. Middle of the week."

"Aw, Addy, you know my schedule…"

"And—" she'd save the best for last "—you can only drink Old Style. Three cans, minimum."

"Cans?" When he grimaced and gave a wistful glance to where his glass of cabernet rested on the table, she knew she'd hurt him.

"Giving up?"

"Not a chance." He toasted her with the wineglass. "I'm sure my stomach will eventually recover. Here's to new experiences."

She leaned forward to clink her bottle against his crystal glass and covered up her frown by taking a sip.

Damn. Now she was going to have to go out and buy a dress.

Addy had always prided herself on knowing where her skills lay and knowing how to delegate authority. The combination of these two traits meant she knew exactly what to do in this crisis.

She called Maxie.

Her sister met her at lunchtime on the corner of Michigan Avenue and Oak Street, the mecca of Chicago for high-end shoppers. Maxie strolled up arm in arm with Sarah. They kissed hello and Addy said she was glad that Sarah was joining them.

"I brought her—" Maxie jerked her head at Sarah "—so you'll believe me when I tell you that you look stunning in floor-length crimson satin. I don't want you trying to run home with a boring black tea dress."

"I don't even know what a tea dress is," Addy moaned, already dreading the idea.

"Then you're lucky I do. Let's shop."

"Okay, but I only have an hour."

Maxie stopped dead in her tracks and looked at her in disbelief. She pulled Addy's backpack off her shoulder, rummaged in it for a moment and dug out the cell phone. She handed it to Addy.

"Cancel your afternoon appointments. Now. I'm not screwing around here."

In the end, Addy decided that it hadn't been too awful. If not for the frequent moments of finding herself standing in her underwear—thank god she'd worn some—in a room with her sisters and various other strange women, listening to them analyze her body and what would look good on it, she might even have found it fun. And the dress she'd gone home with was certainly not black or boring.

The night of the event, she stood in front of her bathroom mirror, struggling with her earrings—she couldn't remember the last time she'd worn earrings—and wobbling on one high heel–shod foot as she tapped around blindly with the other toe on the floor, looking for the second shoe by touch. Spencer was waiting downstairs and she was late.

She managed to get the earring in, a thin dangling bar of brushed gold, at the same moment that her toes found the other shoe. She stepped back and looked at herself in the mirror. Her feet already hurt. *Suffering for beauty,* Maxie called it.

She hoped it was worth it. She'd be limping again by the time the night was over.

Her reflection stared back at her. Strange. She recognized herself, but it was as if someone had stripped her down to the skin and then superimposed the look of another woman over her bare body. Her hair, normally wild with tangled curls, was pulled back in a simple knot at the nape of her neck. Careful makeup made her eyes seem enormously dark, while her lips were stained a deep wine color. The dress, a warm, deep burgundy with a subtle sheen of gold, fell from a thin strip of fabric on her left shoulder in a low drape across her breasts and a lower drape on her back in a clean sweep to the floor. The slight flare toward the bottom would allow her to walk normally, her sisters had promised.

She gave herself a wake-up shake and then double-checked to make sure her dress hadn't fallen off. Time to go.

Two steps out the bathroom door, she turned back. She took the men's watch off her wrist and left it on the counter. Grabbing her ridiculously tiny clutch purse and the matching silk shawl she was sure would do nothing to keep her warm, she headed downstairs.

From the top of the stairs, she spied Spencer glancing at his watch. When he put one foot on the first step, she knew he was coming up to get her. She cleared her throat gently. He turned and looked up. Then took a step backward, staring.

She walked carefully down the stairs, feeling like Cinderella making her entrance at the ball. From the look on Spencer's face, she came to the conclusion that this was not at all a bad thing. Maybe she should try to do this dressing-up thing more often.

At the bottom, she stopped in front of him. She'd been afraid to find him in a tux, which would remind her too much of a prom. But he was perfect in a black suit with a dark gray shirt and darker tie. He raised a hand to her, palm up, and she placed her fingers on his. When he drew her hand to his mouth and pressed his lips to her knuckles, his eyes never left hers. The silent moment made her so tense that she finally laughed, not wanting to take herself too seriously.

He smiled at her without a word and lifted her hand up, turning her in a slow circle in front of him. Three hundred and sixty degrees later, she was a little dizzy and the silence was killing her.

He saved her, as always.

"You're beautiful." He trailed a finger against her neck, across her bare shoulder and down the length of her arm. "Overwhelmingly so."

She knew she was blushing and searched for something to say to lighten the moment. Once again, he had the words she didn't.

His brow quirked and she could see him stifling a grin as he asked his question.

"What exactly is holding that dress up?"

"You don't want to know." She'd been amazed by the tricks Maxie had taught her. "Suffice to say, it might as well be chewing gum."

"And what's underneath it?"

That one she knew how to answer. She took a step forward and pressed herself against him while she drew his head down to whisper in his ear.

"You know I always go commando, baby."

She remembered for the rest of the night his groan and the low laugh that followed it. When he handed her the single rose whose color matched her dress, or handed her into the limo waiting outside the house, she kept those sounds in her mind and told herself not to be nervous. Introductions to the second couple over champagne in the lobby outside their box seats passed in a blur. Before she knew it, the house lights were dimming and they were sitting down in velvet-covered chairs.

She glanced down at the program in her hand as the enormous room fell silent. The first piece was by Bach, a double violin concerto—words that meant absolutely nothing to her.

Then the music began and she forgot that she didn't know what she was listening to.

The two solo violinists stood at the front of the stage before an orchestra that barely registered with her. Their bows flashed with movement. Their fingers danced wildly over strings, their heads nodded strongly with the music. And she could *hear* it.

She could hear them dancing.

One violin chased the melody high and then higher still, the music of the other violin spiraling beneath as the sound of the first tumbled over the top and fell rippling down until the music rose again and the second violin pushed the sound higher. Sometimes they dueled, each topping the other in rapid succession, and then they flirted, melodic fencing with one instrument chasing the other's music. When they slowed and the battling melodies turned into lovers, one sound sliding and curving around the other, she blinked and felt the tears spill at the beauty of it.

She felt Spencer take her hand in his, lace his fingers with hers, but she didn't look at him. Just held on tight.

The final movement jumped into sudden life. In her mind's eye she saw her great-aunt, young and passionate as the musicians on the stage, bent with fire over the violin that now hung on Addy's wall. Addy's breath caught in pain and her heart ached. The music was rushing to a finale she could feel in the tips of her fingers. When the last notes came to a sudden, perfectly timed halt, she was too stunned to applaud.

She felt the pressure on her arm as Spencer leaned over to her. "I'm thinking about her, too."

Addy shook her head. She didn't want to talk about it. That anyone could give this up…

When the music started again, she gave herself up to it and pushed all thoughts of the woman who'd abandoned her music, and Addy's mother, down deep. By the time the musicians took their bows to crashing applause, she joined in the clapping, feeling only her enjoyment of the sound.

Even dinner turned out to be more than pleasant, the older couple they were out with being both charming and funny. When they said good-night and Addy told them she was glad to have met them, she meant it. And in the limo, too much champagne making her sleepy, she didn't hesitate to curl up against Spencer's side as he stroked her arm gently.

"Maybe I'm a little bit of a symphony girl," she admitted in a whisper to his lapel. His hand squeezed her shoulder.

He held her hand entering their home and she walked with him up the stairs. At the top, she moved toward his room, willing for once—no, wanting—to enter it with him, but his hand pulled her in the other direction and she walked down the length of the hallway to her bedroom.

They'd never made love in her room. She stood with him next to her bed and reached up behind her head to undo the knot of her hair. It spilled out over her shoulders and she dropped the pins to the floor. He helped her lift the dress off over her head and then it, too, fell to the floor. Then she helped him undress, until he stood as naked before her as she stood before him.

They lay down on her bed and she moved with him, so slowly that the world seemed to stop on its axis and pause for them. She told him that his hands on her touched her the way the music had, and his kiss on the trembling skin of her stomach spoke of something more than sex. When she fell apart in his arms, he held her. When she felt herself drifting into sleep, she held him.

And knew that he wouldn't leave her before the morning.

Nine

When the shriek of her alarm blasted her out of sound sleep the next morning, Addy bolted out from under the covers, certain she was late for a meeting. The strong grip on her ankle nearly tumbled her onto the floor.

Disoriented, naked and half falling off the bed, she craned her neck around and spotted the trouble. She narrowed her eyes.

"Trouble." And indeed he was, lying there on his side, head propped on one hand and smiling in appreciation at the sight of her. Then she caught sight of the alarm clock suddenly silent under his other hand, and her grumbles transformed into shrieks.

"It's six o'clock! In the morning!" She double-checked the days of the week in her head. "On a Saturday!"

"Yes it is."

She flopped over on her back and spoke to the ceiling.

"So, Judge, sir, can you really consider it intentional homicide, considering the circumstances?" She answered herself as she felt the bed shaking at her side. "No, Ms. Tyler, you cannot. In fact, one can only consider it to have been involuntary manslaughter, at best." She nodded, feeling righteous. "Thank you, Judge. I knew you'd see it my way."

Then she flung an arm over her face and tried to block out the light.

"Easy, Counselor." He rolled on top of her and pulled her arm down. She looked to the right and then the left. Anything to avoid his traitor's face. Then she thought better and looked him in the eye for one last glimpse of him.

After all, he'd be dead soon.

Even sooner if he didn't stop grinning at her.

"Aren't you supposed to be the one who hates mornings?" she asked grumpily.

"I thought I'd wake you up early. Show you one of the benefits of what we grown-ups like to call 'sleepovers.'"

"What's that?"

He dragged blunt fingernails slowly down her side until his fingers rested on the flesh of her hip, flexing his hand on the joint between hip and thigh. She felt herself catching fire from his touch.

"Morning sex."

The benefits of which, she was willing to concede a half hour later, were considerable.

Addy was halfway through her second coat of paint on the upstairs bathroom that afternoon before she realized that by startling her out of sleep and turning the moment playful, he'd managed to take the hour she'd dreaded and make her enjoy it. He'd given her yet another gift.

"Spencer Reed," she said aloud, leaning her head against the wall—a spot not yet painted, thank God, she thought a moment later. She felt as old, or older than, the hills. "You'll be the death of me yet."

And just like that, their patterns shifted again.

Like a light switch flipping from off to on, her desire for him, her need to have him naked and in bed—preferably, but she'd settle for just naked and anywhere—went from being something she could confine to the middle of the night to a constant obsession. Instead of being cautiously glad when their schedules limited the time they could spend together, she found herself becoming remarkably cranky if she left without talking to him in the morning and returned home to find that he was still out.

On one of the late nights when she stayed up, fighting sleep to be awake when he finally came home, she finished *Pride and Prejudice*. She slammed the cover shut with a loud clap and tossed the book to the floor, not sure what she was more irritated with: Spencer's absence, the storybook happy ending or the ridiculous misunderstandings Elizabeth and Darcy went through because they couldn't see each other clearly.

"Novels," she muttered, before shutting off the light and trying to sleep. She was still awake when Spencer came home and into her bed.

And if their schedules weren't bad enough, her family was worse.

After weeks of giving the "couple" plenty of alone time at home, it now seemed that they were determined to drop by at all hours and it took forever to get them to leave.

First Maxie showed up, in tears at having broken up with a boyfriend Addy didn't even remember hearing about. She needed an entire night of tissues and red wine to get her through the weeping and out the other side, where the absurdity of dating an actor who was entirely *too close* to his co-leading man could make her giggle again.

Her brother came by after confronting the pub's owner with his manager's embezzlement, wondering if he'd be looking for a new job soon and looking for sympathy. Even Addy's mother stopped in, after Spencer apparently had mentioned to her on the phone how much he'd loved the jambalaya all those Sundays ago. She brought an enormous pot of the spicy stew over with her, something Addy couldn't remember her doing in all the years that Addy had been living alone, and of course they had to invite Susannah to stay for a while and share it with them.

Meanwhile, Addy wasn't getting laid, frankly, nearly as much as she wanted to. And the worst thing was that her family did all this coming and going without calling first, a habit she'd never had a problem with in the past. But she was seriously considering banning such behavior outright, particularly after Sarah rang their doorbell one Saturday afternoon, approximately two minutes before the view from the door window into the foyer would have gotten extremely interesting.

Not to mention that she still hadn't managed to get Spencer to a Cubs game.

She was standing on the front walk in the dawn hours of a late-May Tuesday morning, drinking Diet Coke and threatening her garden with a fate worse than death if something green didn't start pushing up out of the dirt soon, when she solved that problem at least.

She heard Spencer come out of the house but pretended she didn't, just so she could enjoy the pleasure of him walking up behind her and wrapping his arms around her.

"You can't talk a plant into sprouting for you, love," he said in her ear. She ignored the shiver that ran through her at the casual word.

"Shows what you know," she said and leaned her head back for his kiss. She could smell the scent of coffee on him. "My book says that talking to your houseplants has been proven to make them healthier."

"Putting aside the fact that cursing flowers to eternal damnation is probably not what they meant by talking, can you explain to me what houseplants, with leaves and such, have to do with seeds buried six inches deep in the ground?"

"They're bulbs, thank you," she corrected him and accepted his murmured apologies for blatantly misrepresenting the world of flora. "And, I don't know, they're all part of the same plant family thing, aren't they?"

"Search me."

She spun around in his arms and flung her hands behind his neck.

"There's something else I'd rather do with you."

His hands dropped to her hips and pulled her closer.

"What's that?"

"Watch baseball."

It only took five minutes, full of protests of a busy day on his part and accusations of being a deal welsher on hers, before she talked him into clearing his afternoon in time for them to make the 1:20 p.m. start of the game that day.

On Addison Avenue at one o'clock, she tugged on the hand Spencer held, dragging him through the crowds and urging him to hurry.

"It's bad luck if we miss the national anthem," she scolded as they sprinted across the street against the stoplights, winking at the cop directing traffic. They had already stopped at a bar a block from the ballpark to buy tickets from her favorite scalper. Spencer had looked askance at her when she'd walked up to the tall, grizzled man with broad, bony shoulders leaning against the bar as if he lived there. The man she knew only as Blue greeted her with a smacking kiss and his standard, "Hey there, girlie!"

When Spencer introduced himself as her husband, arm firmly in place around her shoulders, she couldn't sputter out a denial or an explanation fast enough to prevent Blue from making a wedding present of the tickets she wanted.

"You shouldn't have told him that." They were entering the park, still arguing about his possessive gesture.

He wiped a hand across his mouth for the third time. "I can't believe I just did a shot of whiskey at one in the afternoon."

"It was the least I could do after he gave us the tickets." Spencer grunted in reply. "He did offer to let you call the shot, remember. Besides, he went to high school with my dad."

"Lovely."

"For a long while, Blue was the most arrested man in Chicago." She cocked her head, considering. "Not sure if he still holds the title. There are some up-and-coming young ticket scalpers these days."

"Just tell me that you don't kiss them all."

To his credit, once they were inside the park, Spencer followed her every direction without protest. Seated in the bleachers, where there were no individual seats, only numbered tags screwed into benches every sixteen inches, he even seemed to find a silly joy in crowding her, insisting that the man on his left was pushing him over. He stood and cheered with her and the entire stands when Sosa sprinted all the way to the outfield wall at the start of the game. He drank the marginally cold Old Style beer without flinching.

When a five-year-old two rows in front of them—hopped up on cotton candy, cola and hot dogs—threw up in his mom's lap from overexcitement, Spencer didn't even blink. He just casually mentioned that in the box seats there were both waiters and no small children unless one invited them.

She didn't even take her eyes from the field as the opposing team's pitcher wound up and let it rip. A second later, she was on her feet with the rest of the crowd, shouting.

"You call that a strike? Why don't you call your optometrist?"

She looked down at the sound of laughter. The beginnings of a slight sunburn reddened Spencer's cheeks. He was sweating a little in the direct sunlight and smiling up at her. For a moment, the world spun and she braced herself with a hand on his shoulder.

"Okay?" She saw his concern and forced a smile, nodding, and blamed it on the odd feeling she'd had all afternoon. As much as he fit in her world and as much as she'd enjoyed his on the night of the symphony, she was still caught off guard sometimes by how different they were. It was as if seeing double and being unable to determine which vision was the true one.

His hand under her elbow eased her down. "A shot of whiskey at one in the afternoon can have that effect."

She swallowed at the thought and shrugged it off. "I know."

He raised an eyebrow.

"Even at nineteen I wasn't crazy enough to streak around the block *sober.*"

The frozen lemonade at the vendor's stand suddenly seemed more appealing than beer, though, and she didn't object when he followed her lead.

After the game, they walked over to the pub where her brother tended bar, far enough from the park to avoid the postgame crowds. Calling for pints of water to battle their sun-beaten dehydration, they snagged seats at the far end of the bar, under the television where the sportscasters played out their game analysis on mute. Addy and her brother settled into the comfortable tradition of the analysis of the loss. They explained to Spencer that you couldn't consider yourself a true Cubs fan unless you toughed it out through twice as many lost games as won.

When he asked how many games he'd have to sit through before the Cubbies won one, they pelted him with balled-up napkins.

Cubs talk led to rehashing who'd been the better baseball player in their misspent youths, which led soon enough to sibling rivalry being played out on the seventy-five-cent pool table fronting the bar's plate-glass windows.

After the wager reached best four out of seven, Spencer offered to settle the tie by playing each of them. He proceeded to run the table first on her brother, which made her cackle, and then on Addy herself, which made her scowl as she handed over the ten-buck forfeit. He just winked at her.

"You're not the only one with a misspent youth." When she gaped at him, he grinned and shrugged. "They don't call law school study sessions '*bar* review' for nothing."

She begged off the rematch, pleading sunburn and general exhaustion, and kissed her brother goodbye. Outside the bar, she took a deep breath and pressed a hand to her stomach. Two hot dogs and the peanuts had obviously not been a good idea. She wondered if it would be impolite to burp.

"Sorry to interrupt your winning streak," she apologized to Spencer, "but the smoke was getting to me."

He hailed a passing cab. "I'll trounce you anytime you like, sweetheart." She felt him press a kiss on top of the baseball hat she'd bought for him but ended up wearing. "Let's go home."

At home, they collapsed on the sofa in the library and argued over who was going to get up and go to the kitchen for drinks of the caffeinated sort. After a few rounds, Spencer played what he considered to be the ultimate card.

"*I* drank Old Style."

Addy thought for a moment.

"*I* bought it."

"That, my dear, is not exactly something to brag about." When she pitched one of the many aptly named throw pillows at his head, he fielded it with ease and tucked the pillow under her feet on the sofa before standing up, pressing a quick kiss on her mouth and heading to the kitchen. She could hear him from where she lay reclined in the early summer sun, a cool breeze carrying the scent of cut grass through the open window. He was on the phone, ordering a pizza for dinner. His dinner at least, since the thought of food still made her stomach do a slow backflip.

She called out to him and he carried the phone with him as he came back into the room.

"Will you skip the green peppers tonight, please?" she asked. At his curious glance, she explained. "My stomach's still out of whack and the thought of that smell—" she grimaced "—yech. Sorry."

When he sat down again next to her and pulled her feet onto his lap, unlacing her shoes and starting a slow, deep foot massage, she could have groaned out loud. She draped her head over the sofa arm and gave in to the urge.

"God, I like you so much."

"You're just saying that because I'm rubbing your feet. See how much you like me when I make you get up and answer the door when the pizza gets here."

She barely heard him, although his words reassured her that he hadn't noticed the tiny little stumble she'd made, the brief hesitation before she'd managed to finish her sentence by saying "*like* you so much."

She had been on the verge of saying, "God, I love you."

Maybe she could have played it off. After all, people said "I love you" all the time and didn't mean it. She'd said it herself yesterday to a co-worker who'd brought two dozen doughnuts to the office. And she certainly didn't have any deep personal feelings for Susie LeClerc beyond gratitude for the snack on a day with no time for a lunch break.

But he would only have needed one look at her face, frozen with shock at the sound of her own words, to make the truth abundantly clear.

She was in love with him. In love with her husband, and that made everything completely and horribly wrong.

Spencer was still stroking the arch of her feet with his thumbs, kneading deep and then manipulating her heel. She wondered that it didn't vibrate under his fingers with the tension that hummed through her. He seemed to think she had fallen asleep, which was fine. It gave her time to think.

She couldn't think.

What the hell was she supposed to do now?

Sure, Spencer was the one who had brought up the idea of their staying married once or twice in the past, but that was a long time ago. And he'd meant it more as a matter of convenience between the two of them, since they'd both been burned before. She didn't think he'd appreciate it if she sat up now and turned to him, saying, "You know, let's do it. Let's stay married. We share a house well enough, sex is clearly not a problem and by the way, do you love me?"

Yeah. Right. No way. Her heart was already racing with dread at the thought.

Calm down, girl, she told herself. Don't go getting all agitated here. Just take a page from the book of the man himself. Spencer Reed's Guide to the Calm and Reasonable Approach to Any Crisis.

There was no law requiring her to make any kind of immediate confession of her feelings to Spencer. She could simply tuck them away for now and let things just ride for a while. He'd said something similar to her once, she remembered, about the possibility of their hitting the six-month goal line and letting things go from there. So she'd crossed a line of her own, and considerably before the six months were up, too. So what?

She would just let it go from here. No expectations, no pressure. After all, the man liked her, she knew that. He made efforts to see that she was happy, although frankly she explained some of that away by picturing his mother as a dragon lady who'd locked him in a closet as a child if he'd failed to be polite. But surely there was a chance at least that someday it might be more than politeness that motivated his concern for her.

She knew she would never get the grand, overwhelming declaration of eternal love. Spencer just wasn't the type. But there was something to be said for a man who brought her Ace bandages when she sprained her ankle and Diet Coke at any and all hours of the day. That kind of man would never wake up one day and decide that the grand-gesture thing was getting a little old, and leave.

The kind of man Spencer was would find little ways of making her happy every day, for all of their days, and maybe that was better.

Certainly it was better.

That resolved, she opened her eyes and found Spencer watching her. God, she loved the look of him. The dimple that showed up in one long, lean cheek when he smiled. The solid shape of muscles under his clothes that made it feel like a secret when she pictured him naked. His quick smile. The horn-rimmed glasses he used only for reading.

He wiggled one of her toes.

"Had a nice nap?"

"Mmm."

She pulled her feet off his lap, rose to her knees next to him and swung a leg over his thighs, straddling him. Bent her head and started working on the tiny buttons of his white oxford shirt.

"That must have been some nap."

Addy pushed his head back until it rested on the couch, and leaned above him. His hands ran up the back of her thighs, up and under the hem of the khaki shorts she wore, as she lowered her mouth with torturous slowness over his. She kissed him, lips soft and open, first on one side of his mouth and then the other, and ran her fingers through his silky hair just for the pleasure of feeling it in her hands.

"I just thought I'd show you one of the benefits of what we Cubs fans like to call the 'postgame blues.'"

His hands kneading firmly against her butt, he was grinning up at her before she finished.

"What's that?"

She was on her knees above his lap, her chest level with his face, as she crossed her arms, gripped the hem of her shirt and pulled it off, knocking off her ball cap on the way and spilling her hair out of the loose ponytail she'd pulled through the back of the cap. His blue-sky eyes clouded and narrowed as she ran a hand down her own bare skin, fingers stroking her own throat, trailing between her breasts, falling, falling, until her hand rested on the top button of her shorts.

She felt a little bit wicked as she popped the button out of the buttonhole and answered him. "Comfort sex."

Their mouths met, mated, and he slid his hands farther up her shorts. The wet readiness of her wrung a groan from him as he plunged a finger inside her. His other hand streaked up her naked back to tangle in the ends of her hair, pulling her head back and pushing her bare breasts forward.

When the frustration grew to be too much, Spencer pushed her off his lap to stand up and rapidly tugged her shorts down. She pulled him up off the couch and his clothes were gone in a moment. His skin was hot against her as she curled one arm around his neck and stroked a hand over the hard, smooth surface of his chest and the flatness of his stomach. She ran her hand down his side, his hair-roughened outer thigh with its long muscles and then back up the inside until she cupped him in her hands.

Her fingers stroked the length of him, and the force of will that let him stand still as she touched him made him tremble against her.

His hand tightened on the nape of her neck and his forehead pressed against hers as she drew a low moan from him with her fingers.

When she pushed him back down on the couch, he tried to pull her with him, but she dodged his hands. She had something else in mind.

She dropped to her knees and took him in her mouth. Felt him shudder beneath her hands as she loved him. When his every muscle bunched and she felt the energy near to exploding under his skin, he hauled her bodily up over him and pushed her hips down, burying himself inside of her. She curved above him, one knee on the couch, one foot braced on the floor, and felt his hands touching her where their bodies joined, his thumb stroking her until she trembled and shoved herself in strong, rolling thrusts against him.

When she came and cried out, he lifted his hips beneath her, once, twice, until his climax overtook him and he groaned, his breath mingling with hers under the dark curtain of her hair as it fell around them.

She was still panting to get her breath back as he scooted over and tucked her against his side in the space between his body and the sofa back. She lay on her side, threw a leg over his and draped an arm across his. Her fingers dangling over the edge of the couch found his arm and began tracing random patterns on the soft skin on the inside of his elbow. Her head rested on his shoulder.

When she felt him shake his head after a moment, she made a little noise of inquiry.

"So," he began, and the laugher was so full in his voice that she tilted her head back to look up at him. "Do you feel better about the Cubs' loss today?" He threw his head back and laughed out loud. "Jeez, I sure do."

Since he was laughing already, it seemed the perfect time to poke him in the side with a stiff finger. That she managed to tickle him was completely an accident, she swore, as Spencer dumped her on the floor, grabbed her wrists and threatened to tickle her until she peed.

The doorbell rang insistently and she gasped with relief as he let up. They both remembered about the pizza at the same instant.

"Oh, damn. Oh, damn." She hopped about until she got both feet out of the same leg of her shorts and managed to yank them up over her hips. Spencer was sitting naked on the floor in the middle of the room, laughing uproariously at her and wiping tears out of his eyes.

"You are not helping," she informed him, and abandoned the search for her top as the guy at the door gave up on subtlety and just leaned on the buzzer. She grabbed Spencer's discarded shirt and the wallet from his pants and sprinted down the hall, shoving buttons through holes any which way.

By the time she yanked open the front door, she'd managed two buttons, but the shirt was barely hanging on one shoulder and she was pretty sure the teenage delivery boy could tell that she wasn't wearing a bra.

Who was she fooling? By the look in his pubescent eyes, he knew perfectly well that she'd just been having sex.

She thrust an extra twenty at him out of sheer embarrassment, grabbed the pizza box out of his hands and closed the door in his face. Then she sagged against the door in relief.

When she heard a muffled, "Man, what a babe" through the door, followed by footsteps trailing away, she was only marginally consoled.

Spencer had his pants back on by the time she returned to the library, and a contrite expression on his face that lasted about three seconds when she frowned at him. He dissolved into laughter again, walked up and wrapped his arms around her. She balanced the pizza box on one hand, out of reach.

"I'm sorry. I'm not laughing at you, I promise." He buried his face in the crook of her neck and snorted. "I've just never seen anyone move that fast."

When she felt the hands at her side twitch on her ribs, she gave in.

"No more tickling! You can *have* the pizza!"

He swept the box out of her hands and smacked a kiss on her mouth.

They sat cross-legged on the floor on opposite sides of the coffee table, munching away and talking lazily about what they had to do tomorrow. Addy discovered that she finally had an appetite again and plowed her way through several slices.

Spencer asked her what her plans were for the following evening.

"Finishing the bathroom," she mumbled around a mouthful of cheese before licking her fingers. "It's going to be too nice out this weekend to be stuck inside painting trim."

"The paint job turned out great, by the way." He handed her a napkin.

"Thanks. And thanks." She took it. "I love messing around with that stuff. It just never seemed worth it before in a rented apartment."

"Well, you'll certainly have your chance now." The flick of his gaze at the ceiling encompassed the house that surrounded them.

"Yeah, thanks to you." At his shrug of denial, she reached across the table, grabbing his fingers and squeezing his knuckles together. "I mean it. I don't know if I've ever actually said it, but thank you. Thank you for marrying me. This is more important to me than you could know."

As usual, he didn't let her get away with stopping short of the full explanation. Pushing the coffee table to the side, he scooted around until he faced the same direction as her. Then he slung an arm around her shoulder and pulled her back to lean with him against the front of the couch. He pressed a kiss on the top of her head as he settled back with a comfortable exhale.

"So tell me why it's so important."

To her surprise, she found herself doing exactly that. Although her voice halted at first, she told him about her childhood after her father died. How at eight years old, she'd been the only person her mother had to depend on for help with the three younger children. How the toes of her gym shoes had had holes worn in them for months because she hadn't wanted to tell her mother that she'd outgrown them, knowing that each new expense pushed her mother closer to the edge of being unable to make their rent payment.

"By the time I was in high school, things were pretty stable. I was a fairly normal teenager, with a pitiful allowance and babysitting duties at home after school, but I knew that at least we were safe." She shifted her upper body so that she rested more securely against Spencer. "God, it'd kill my mother to know that I still think about those days. That my definition of safety is knowing I have a roof over my head that no one can take away from me."

"That must have been a scary way to grow up."

She shrugged, not willing to admit that. She slid the crust of her last slice to Elwood, who'd snuck into the room at the scent of hot food. "Maybe. But I wanted to help her. And it was nice sometimes to feel needed."

"And now you have this house."

"Are you trying to jinx me?" she asked, looking up at him. She rapped her knuckles lightly against his forehead. "Knock on wood. Nothing's for sure until it's over. We could get overrun by a plague of termites tomorrow that chew the house down to the foundation overnight."

"Unlikely in the extreme."

"It happened to a woman in Tennessee last summer."

"Where did you hear that?"

"It was on the Internet."

"You *do* know that not everything on the Internet is true, right?"

"What?"

When Spencer began lecturing her on evaluating the reliability of information sources, Addy shut him up with a kiss that led to her proving that she knew how to retrieve reliable information from some sources very well indeed. Her research was exhaustive and ended with their naked bodies sprawled crosswise on her bed.

Spencer conceded that in some areas she was indeed very well informed.

The room was dark when she woke out of sound sleep hours later, unsure of what had awakened her. A sudden surge of nausea answered that question with emphasis. She bolted for her bathroom.

Torn between trying not to wake Spencer and trying not to lose her dinner on the floor, she didn't waste time closing the door but didn't turn on the light, either. Reaching the toilet, she lost the contents of her stomach in gut-wrenching spasms that left her stomach muscles sore when at last she finished, panting in the dark. She closed the door and switched on the light before stumbling to the sink to rinse her mouth and brush her teeth. Her face was pale and sweaty in the mirror, her eyes enormously dark.

The fear she'd blocked from conscious thought for days now was demanding to be heard.

She had a mouthful of spit and toothpaste when the door opened behind her and Spencer entered the bathroom. He'd pulled pants on but hadn't bothered to zip them.

"Are you okay?"

She turned her back on him, bent over the sink and spit. Raising her head, she swiped a hand over her mouth and looked at his reflection instead of facing him.

"No. I think I'm pregnant."

Ten

"**H**ow long have you known?"

She slammed another bureau drawer closed. All she wanted was a pair of sweatpants, damn it. How come nothing was ever where it was supposed to be?

"I figured it out about thirty seconds ago."

Out of the corner of her eye, she could see him, backlit in the doorway to the bathroom. She was rummaging in the dark in the bedroom because suddenly she didn't want to stand naked in the light before him.

"And before?"

His voice was calm, neutral, but she heard the words as an accusation.

Finally, sweatpants. Sweatshirts. She settled the thick, roomy clothes on her frame and felt more protected. Not much, but some.

"Before? Before, I didn't want to know," she said. She felt around on top of the bureau until she found a scrunchie, then scraped her hair back into a tight ponytail. The need to feel in control of things was overwhelming. "I could barely admit I was sleeping with you, much less that I might be pregnant."

"Because that would be a bad thing?"

"Jesus, Spencer! Of course it's a bad thing!" She was shouting at him now as the fear made her heart race and broke her mind into little tiny pieces that whirled in circles. Turning her back to him, she stared into the empty, dark room. Wrapped her hands around her middle and hunched her shoulders. God, her stomach ached.

When he came up behind her and tried to make her lean back against him, she didn't bend.

"Stomach still hurt? Can I get you anything?" He rubbed her shoulder.

She didn't want to be soothed, damn it.

"I'm not an invalid," she said stiffly and broke away from his touch. "I'll get it myself."

All the way down to the kitchen, she could hear him behind her. The sound of his footsteps made her feel trapped. Why couldn't he leave her alone for two minutes so she could try to figure out what she was going to do now?

In the kitchen, she tugged the refrigerator door open, the light making her blink, and grabbed a two-liter of Diet Coke. Unscrewing the cap, she swigged straight from the bottle.

"Addy, do you think that's—"

"Good for the baby?" She slammed the fridge door and took another defiant swallow. Felt the coldness and the bubbles clean her mouth and settle her stomach. "I'll tell you what, Reed. As soon as you start puking your guts out, you can tell me what I need to feel better."

"Okay."

"And stop being so reasonable, would you?"

He stepped in front of her and grabbed her by the shoulders, hunching over to force her to look at him when she wouldn't raise her eyes. He shook her gently for emphasis.

"I'm on your side, Addy." When she still wouldn't look at him, he stood up and, sighing, wrapped her and the Diet Coke bottle in a hug against his bare chest. His skin was warm on her cheek. "I love you."

She heard the words both out loud and as the vibration that hummed in his chest along with the thump of his heartbeat. Her face was wet, her breath ragged.

"I love you," he said again, and it hurt worse the second time.

She leaned against him for one moment more. How she would have given anything to hear those words just a few hours ago. When she pulled away from him, it was as if she were slowly ripping herself in half.

She could look at him now, because she loved him so much for what he would try to do for her. Lifting a hand to his face, she shook her head. "No, you don't."

Before he could speak, she covered his lips with her fingers to stop him. "We've been together for weeks now, and you decide that you love me five minutes after you find out I'm going to have your baby?" Her voice was gentle. She wasn't trying to wound him now. "I remember how much you said you wanted to have children. How your other relationships ended when you realized those women didn't want the same thing. And I'm glad. Glad that you will love this child." She dropped her hand. "But that's not the same as being in love with me."

His arms hung at his sides, hands clenching into fists and then opening wide in a slow rhythm. She knew he wanted to shake her—it was easy to read the anger in the set of his shoulders and the thinness of his lips, even if good breeding kept him from letting it show in his voice.

"So you're saying I'm lying to you."

She laughed shortly. "No, that wouldn't be polite. I'm sure you believe it when you say you love me." Her voice caught on the last three words. "But I think you're lying to yourself."

If she thought she'd seen him in control of his emotions before, that was nothing compared to the way he shut down in front of her. Like a sharp blade scraping over glass, his face cleared of all expression.

"Apparently your great-aunt was correct and I have been giving you too much credit for possessing some measure of rationality." The words dropped like individual cubes snapped frozen from the tray. "Or maybe this has been your plan from the beginning? After all, the property taxes alone on this house would beggar you. Unless of course you had the ability to call on someone with money. A lot of money."

It took her a moment to figure out what he'd accused her of. When she did, her hand flew out of its own accord.

To be stopped in midair by his strong grip on her wrist.

"Careful, Addy. You'll want to make good and sure you're pregnant before you go alienating me completely." His smile scoured her raw. "No, wait. You've already done that."

He left the room.

Addy wasn't sure how long she stood stranded in the middle of the kitchen floor before moving again. Long enough to feel a glacial coldness grind over her and settle in.

Upstairs, for the first time since she'd come to live there, she wished there was a lock on the door to her room. She set the cola bottle carefully on the nightstand, pulled back the covers and climbed into bed. She was shivering, shaking with cold, and the blanket she wrapped tightly around her couldn't seem to warm her. There was a pain in her chest and she couldn't catch her breath as she curled up around a pillow and stared into the dark. She could have wept, because her heart was breaking.

She could have thrown a brick through the window, she was so angry.

At dawn, she left the house and went to her mother's.

She stood shivering on the front steps in the chilly mist of the early morning as she waited for her mother to respond to the buzzer.

When she did and the door opened, it took only one look on her part.

"Oh, baby," Susannah said and pulled her daughter into an

embrace. Addy stumbled blindly into her arms, palms pressed against her eyes to hold back the tears that would not stop. With her mother's arms wrapped around her, hands stroking her hair, Addy struggled to explain. The words broke off in ragged chunks between desperate gasping breaths. "I thought. It would feel better. To leave. Even just a little." She couldn't catch her breath. There was a pain in her chest as if she would die. "But it doesn't. It feels sad. And lonely." Her eyes ached. Her nose was running. The pounding in her head was so loud. "I'm so lonely, Mama."

"Shh. I know." And Addy held on.

An hour later, she was curled up on the couch in the living room, an old, worn afghan draped around her in an effort to stop the chills that still rolled over her. She still couldn't get warm. The coffee mug she cradled between her palms—decaf, on her mother's orders—warmed her hands but little else.

She'd wanted it for the smell, hoping she would feel her father with her, but it only made her think of Spencer, who hadn't come after her as she'd left the house. She knew it was foolish to want that. It seemed she was indeed as foolish as he thought her.

"What are you going to do now?" Her mother sat beside her on the couch.

"Today? Call in sick to work?" She let out half a laugh. Her hair was down and she ran a tired hand through it. It was daylight out, which seemed strange. Time for her felt as though it had stopped. "After that, I don't know. Go home, I guess. To my apartment," she added at Susannah's look. "I can't go back to that house."

"You can stay here if you want."

"Thanks." She stretched a hand out of the cocoon of her blanket and tangled her fingers with her mother's. "I might. But can we keep everyone away for a bit?" She was thinking of her brother and sisters, not feeling up to the questions they would ask.

"Only for a few days, sweetie." Susannah's lips curved in

a gentle smile. "If we don't let them in for dinner on Sunday, they're going to know something's wrong."

"God, they'll break down the door." She laughed for the first time in what felt like her entire life.

Silence rested easily between them for a while longer.

"And the baby?"

She'd told her mother everything in the last hour.

"I want it," was her simple answer. Beneath the blanket, she spread a hand across the stretch of her flat stomach and knew that much was sure. She looked at her mother, the dark eyes and the curling hair so similar to her own, and hoped she would be as strong and beautiful in twenty years. "I already love it as much as you must have loved me."

To her surprise, Susannah frowned and seemed to hesitate before she spoke.

"I don't know, Addy. Did I love you enough?"

"What are you talking about?" She was getting nervous now. This was a ridiculous line of conversation. "You loved me plenty. I've never doubted that. Ever."

"If you knew what it felt like to have me love you, then how come you don't recognize the same thing in Spencer?"

"Because it's not the same." She set her coffee mug on the table in front of the couch. Smiled an apology when her mother reached over and slid a coaster beneath the warm ceramic. "Spencer cares—cared—about me, I know. And he'll love his child with all his heart."

"But?"

The tears were gathering again. She tipped her head back a little to stop them falling. After she blinked for a moment, she could sit up straight again.

"But it turns out that I *am* the love-letter type." Her breathing hitched. She let out a long slow exhale. Her words wouldn't make sense to her mother. "I needed more than someone who just wanted to do the right thing."

Addy stayed at her mother's house for two days and let her mother answer the phone when it rang and the doorbell when it buzzed. It was never who Addy wanted it to be, anyway. Spencer didn't call or come by. On the third day, she dug out the key chain that she hadn't used in three months and went back to her old apartment.

In the days that followed, she learned to live alone again. To sleep by herself in a bed without waking up in the middle of the night because she was reaching for someone who wasn't there. When she woke up now in the night, it was usually because she needed to run to the bathroom and throw up.

As it turned out, she hadn't been able to keep her siblings away for more than twenty-four hours.

Her brother had to be sat on, of course, until he crossed his heart and hoped to die and promised not to go back to the big house and pound the crap out of Spencer.

Then Maxie had to be sat on, until she promised not to clean out the north-side shops of every Onesie and T-shirt tagged "newborn."

Sarah just smiled and handed her a copy of *What to Expect When You're Expecting.*

"Not as gripping as *Pride and Prejudice,* I admit, but more useful."

There were hours of conversation. Plans were made and thrown away on a daily basis, and Addy smiled and talked and even sometimes laughed. She spoke of buying a house. She'd been saving for years for just that purpose, after all. But she knew it wasn't just any house that she wanted to fill the hole that gaped wide in her and made her heart stumble in the first moments of the morning when she awoke hoping to find herself in a different room.

She told herself how lucky her child would be to grow up with aunts and an uncle who were already so excited about its arrival that they'd taken to talking directly to Addy's stomach rather than her face.

Telling herself such lies would have been a comfort, if only she could believe any of them.

Although she'd gone back to work after a couple of days,

it was on a Saturday afternoon when her buzzer rang and she opened her door to see the same FedEx man she'd nearly flattened on an icy sidewalk so many ages ago.

He didn't give any sign that he recognized her, but she knew even before she signed for the package and looked at the return address who it was from.

Her hands shook as she tore the cardboard strip off the top of the bulky envelope and dumped the contents on her lap. The sight of a white note card tucked under the rubber band that held closed the covers of an old leather journal had her vision blurring for a minute.

"I found this in the attic and thought that you should have it, at least.

S"

The straight lines of his handwriting, its steep slant, were as familiar to her as the lines on her own palms. She slid the card between the covers of the book and tried to drive away thoughts of the dozens of other cards she'd left behind, still sitting in the sock drawer of the dresser of her room at Great-Aunt Adeline's house.

When the picture refused to go away, she looked at the journal, hoping to distract herself. It was a ledger, mostly filled with lists of monthly accounts. Payments made and received. There were occasional comments in the margin about the weather, a reminder to give the boy who mowed the lawn five dollars on his birthday. The handwriting was spiky and uncertain, at times dipping below the ruled line it traveled. Even without knowing that it had belonged to her great-aunt, Addy would have guessed that the inscriber had been very old.

What she didn't expect to recognize in the pages as she turned them, scanning slowly, was the loneliness.

"Haven't seen the mailman in three days. Hope he's not sick."

Three pages later. "Neighbor's boy came in for cookies after finishing the lawn. He's getting so tall."

There was no mention of anyone who might be a friend. And she knew that there'd been no family left after Adeline had closed the door on her niece, Susannah, for refusing to give up her lover or her baby.

Toward the end, the personal notes grew longer as the accounts dwindled. Addy could feel the isolation growing, pictured an old woman sitting alone at the window of an empty house, watching the hedges grow high and catching the occasional glimpse of the world moving past on the other side of the fence.

The last entry was a long, rambling paragraph, the words scarcely legible.

I dreamed about John last night. Not young, but old. Even older than I am now. His hair was very white and his fingers would not straighten, but he put them on the keyboard of the piano and played it and the sound was the same as the first night I heard him. Such a foolish thing to do, to fall in love with a man thirty years your senior just because his music makes you weep. And to let him fall in love with you when you know you will never have the courage to follow him away from your home, your family. But how could I? My parents were so angry with me for playing onstage that one time. The Chicago Symphony Orchestra might as well have been a band playing in a burlesque show, for all their carrying on about their daughter performing in public. To tell them I was in love with the concertmaster was impossible. He was soon gone, in any case. The symphony toured for two years in Europe, I think. I chose to give up the music, he chose to follow it. Or perhaps the reminders of my betrayal of his trust were just too great in the city where we'd loved each other for a little while and lost ourselves in the melodies. I cannot regret it. My entire life would be worthless, wasted, if I thought I had made the wrong choice and lived with it for the next seventy-five years. I made the only choice possible.

But I dreamed of John last night and wished that I

had played with the symphony just one more time.

I wished that I could have been a little more like Susannah.

Tucked between the last fragile pages of the ledger was a photograph. Addy recognized the fight-the-power clenched fist of the newborn even before she turned the picture over and saw the words written in her mother's firm, sloped handwriting.

Adeline Marie Tyler. One week old.

She smiled at her baby self and pressed a hand to her belly, a gesture that she found herself making a hundred times a day.

Before she could change her mind, she got up and found her backpack. Tearing a sheet of graph paper off the top of the pad she'd pulled out, she scrawled the words *Thank you* across the page on the diagonal, folded it and put it in an envelope. If she were lucky, it would go out in the afternoon mail.

Nothing had changed. It couldn't, not just like that. She wasn't so full of fantasy that ten minutes and the words of an old, lonely woman made her want to jump up and run home to a man who might not even be there for her anymore.

When she heard herself using words like *home* and *might*, she wondered how long it would be before she talked herself out of her resolve.

Late in the night between Sunday and Monday morning, she called Spencer's office to leave him a message. She knew that his voice-mail system would date- and time-stamp her call and he would know that she'd called on purpose when he wouldn't be there, but she didn't care. She wasn't ready to talk to him yet.

The phone ringing in her ear seemed very far away. She was so tired, sleep licking the edge of consciousness. Calling from bed on her cell phone had seemed simpler than going in search of the last place she'd left the portable.

But it was taking forever.

She would just rest her eyes.

When she heard his voice, rough and scratchy as it always was before he woke up completely, she thought she was dreaming.

"Addy?"

How lovely. She could just lie here and listen to him talk. She'd missed the sound of his voice.

"Addy, I know it's you. I have caller ID."

She snapped awake. Definitely not a dream, then.

"Spencer?" she stuttered. What now? "I must have fallen asleep."

"And then called me?" The streets outside were quiet, her neighbors silent above and below her. They might have been the only two souls awake in the city. "Should I be flattered?"

"No. I was awake when I called—" her voice was heavy with sleep "—but the phone just kept ringing." The fog cleared for a moment. She wasn't making any sense. "Why are you still at the office?"

"I'm not. I forwarded all calls to my cell phone so I wouldn't miss you if you called." In the middle of the night, it didn't seem so embarrassing to be caught.

"I'm that predictable? Doesn't sound like an irrational woman." She could have swallowed her tongue as she let the bitter words slip out.

"Ah, Addy." When he sighed, it felt as if he was right next to her. "It's much easier for me to apologize when you're not throwing my words back in my face."

"You don't really expect me to worry about making it easier for you to say you're sorry."

"No, although I do wonder that you don't feel any need to do the same for calling me a liar. Even if only to myself." They were both silent. She heard a faint crackle, a break in the reception of her cell phone. She wasn't sure if he was still there or not, and the freedom of not knowing allowed her to say the words.

"I'm sorry."

"So am I. Very sorry." She heard him laugh softly. "Although I do think it's crazy that you wouldn't believe me. Wouldn't take what I wanted to give you."

She wanted to say it. Could hear herself in her head. *Don't fall asleep. I'll be there in fifteen minutes.*

But she didn't say the words out loud. Just cradled the phone closer to her ear and listened to him breathing. Pictured him doing the same. When she spoke, it was with regret at the hurt she knew she'd be causing.

"I want to come by the house tomorrow to get some things." That wasn't all, and he must have guessed, because he said nothing. "But I don't want you to be there when I do."

The wait before he spoke seemed interminable.

"Fine."

She sighed. That was her man. Ever the reasonable soul. No tantrums or shouting matches or demands that she sit down with him and hash this mess out. Once again, he would do whatever she asked of him.

She should be happy. Instead, she was dumb enough to wish that just once she could be important enough for someone to fight for.

"Thank you." She listened. Silence roared in her ear. She had to hang up. "'Bye."

She lowered the phone and pushed the end button, but she could still hear him saying the words.

"You should have believed me, Addy."

She parked on the street outside the house the next afternoon and pretended she wasn't giving in to the fear that she might need to make a quick getaway. At the door, she hesitated before sliding her key into the lock. It felt as if she were sneaking into a stranger's house. When she opened the door and Elwood came bounding and skidding across the slick entryway floor to greet her, she almost laughed from sheer nerves.

"Who's a good boy?" She bent over the dog, scrubbing her knuckles against his shaggy side and scratching him under the chin. After a moment, she lifted her head.

Great-Aunt Adeline's violin still hung on the wall, the polished sheen of the old wood glowing rosy in the afternoon light. The portrait of a long-dead woman named Susannah, the first thing to have awakened her to her connection to this house, was visible farther down the hallway. A pair of Spencer's running shoes, the laces undone, sat on the bottom step of the staircase.

The tears were already flowing as she stood up and walked briskly up the steps to what had been her bedroom. Stupid hormones. She'd better hurry or she'd be a blubbering mess by the time she managed to get out of there.

In the room itself, she focused on the essentials. No time for a general clearing out. That could wait for a day when she was stronger, a possibility that seemed as remote as her making a spur-of-the-moment decision to climb Mount Everest. Just her work files, the solitary suit in her closet and some socks. She seemed to have no socks back at her apartment.

She was standing over her desk, fingertips running over the lines of the floor plans she'd drawn of the house, when she knew he was in the room with her.

The suit in its dry cleaner's bag, draped over her arm, rustled as she turned around. Spencer stood at the foot of the bed, a sheaf of papers clutched in one hand. In dark gray slacks and a deep blue dress shirt, sleeves rolled up and collar unbuttoned, he looked just like the fancy uptown lawyer whose calls and letters she'd ignored until the day she'd walked into his office and he'd turned her world upside down and shook out the spare change.

Exactly the same. Until she looked in his eyes and saw reflected there the same bone-deep weariness that constantly threatened to overwhelm her. Until she noticed his grip on the papers tighten until they crumpled.

"You promised not to be here," was all she could think to say.

"I lied."

The planes of his cheeks were sharper, as if the skin were stretched tighter over his bones. The slight sunburn he'd had on the day of the Cubs game had faded to a light tan that did nothing to hide the shadows of lost sleep under his eyes.

And, Lord help her, he needed a haircut.

Exactly the same. And yet, as if she was seeing him clearly for the first time. Summer warmth began thawing what had been frozen in her since she'd left.

"Spencer—"

"I've spent every day since you left trying to figure it out. After I got over wanting to strangle you. How to write the perfect love letter to convince you that I love you. The argument that would make you believe me." He ran the fingers of his free hand through already rumpled hair. "Then I thought that maybe I should make some big romantic gesture."

On the foot of the bed next to him, she could see the pile of balled-up socks and the stack of note cards next to it and she knew that the little gestures were the ones she would appreciate most for the rest of her life.

"Do you know what these are?" He shook the stack of papers at her. "Faxes." He peeled off the top sheet and glanced at it. "The Prudential Building will let me spell *Will you marry me, Addy?* in office-window lights for a negotiable fee. I didn't mention that it was a little late for a proposal." He tossed the paper to the floor and took a step toward her. "Wrigley Field says I can put a message in lights on the outfield scoreboard." Another toss and another step. "The North-Side Players will act out a romantic scene for you at your office. They were thinking more like *Sleepless in Seattle,* but promised to do their best with *Pride and Prejudice.*" Toss and a step. "For twenty-five bucks, I can name a star after you." Toss. He was standing so close, she could have touched him. "And then there's the baby's room."

"Spencer, I—"

"Just shut up and look at this." He grabbed her by the arm and pulled her out of the room. Her wrist hurt, he held it so tightly. He flung open the door to one of the spare bedrooms and waved wildly at the interior.

"I did all this and then I wondered if you'd think I was only doing it because I wanted the baby more than I wanted you." The walls of the room were painted a bright honey-yellow. Pooh and Piglet, Eeyore and Tigger, danced around the ceiling. She blinked and the picture swam before her eyes.

"And I don't, Addy."

He shifted his grip on her wrist and pulled her hand to his chest, pressing it flat against his heart. Waited until she looked back at him. His eyes held her, and the love in them was all for her, she knew.

"I don't want you because you're pregnant. And I don't want you because we get along okay and the sex is all right." She snuffled out a laugh and curled her fingers under his. "I'm not interested in just letting things ride, Addy, to see where they take us. I love you and I need you with me, and if I have to tie you to a damn chair and shout that at you until you believe it, I will."

He was shouting at her. And she was crying now, because she'd never heard anything more wonderful.

She fumbled over his mouth with her fingers, found his lips. He needed to shut up now.

"Okay."

He stared at her, as if waiting for her to speak English. After a minute he said, "Maybe you could make it clear what you're saying okay to. I want to be sure."

God, she loved this man.

"I'm saying it's okay." She linked her arms around his neck and pulled his face down to hers. "I love you, too."

The wall broke and his mouth fell on her, kissing her lips, her cheeks, her hair, hands fisting in the back of her shirt as if he was afraid she might yet step away from him. She leaned against him, her rock, the one who would always be there for her, and kissed him back, saying the words again and again, until he buried his face in her hair, eased his grip and hugged her to his chest.

"Thank God." His words were muffled. A laugh hiccuped out of her.

"You knew I'd say that."

She felt him shake his head. "I hoped."

Pressing a kiss on the warm skin of his neck, she whispered in his ear. "I'll say it whenever you like."

"Always."

She smiled. "I love you."

"I have a confession to make," he whispered in her ear a second later.

"What's that?" she whispered back.

When he stood up and leaned back against her clasped hands, she was surprised to see that he was blushing.

"I have lied to you once before."

"I knew it. You don't really like all those vegetables on your pizza."

"No. Shush." He stroked the curls back off her face. "Do you remember Steve Henderson?"

She flipped through her mental files. "The bigamist? What'd he do now?"

"He got married…" What did that have to do with anything? She figured it out when he finished with, "…for the first time."

Pause. "You mean he wasn't…"

"No." He grinned at her guiltily and lifted his shoulders for a second. She reared back and punched him in the shoulder.

"Oh, my God." She punched him again. "Oh, my God! Do you know how many people I told about that?"

He trapped her arms with his and hugged her again, rocking back and forth as she cursed him, and he laughed out loud. He did have one suggestion for her, though.

"Maybe we can put a postscript on the wedding announcement."

She pictured it and shook her head.

"Baby, you're going to have write it in lights on that outfield scoreboard to get me out of this one."

"And I hope they charge you by the letter."

* * *

It was the strangest thing they'd ever seen, most of the thirty-six thousand fans at the Cubs Fourth of July night game agreed among themselves later that summer. During the seventh-inning stretch, right after the mayor led the crowd in singing "Take Me Out to the Ballgame," a message in blinking white lights scrolled across the scoreboard.

Thank you, Adeline Marie Tyler Spencer, for marrying me. And sincere apologies to Steve Henderson, who is not, in fact, a bigamist.

Everyone remembered that for a very long time. Not the least, Caroline Reed, who claimed to have heard her father whisper the words while resting his cheek against her mother's belly six months before she was born.

* * * * *

Silhouette®

Desire®

Coming in May 2005
from Silhouette Desire

DYNASTIES : THE ASHTONS

A family built on lies…brought together
by dark, passionate secrets.

Nalini Singh's
AWAKEN THE SENSES
(Silhouette Desire #1651)

Charlotte Ashton was quiet and shy, but to
renowned winemaker Alexandre Dupre, she was
an intriguing challenge. Charlotte's guarded ways
had him wanting to awaken her senses, and pretty
soon Alexandre was too tempting to resist.

Available at your favorite retail outlet.

If you enjoyed what you just read,
then we've got an offer you can't resist!

Take 2 bestselling
love stories FREE!
Plus get a FREE surprise gift!

Brenda Jackson

and Silhouette Desire present a hot new romance starring another sexy Westmoreland man!

JARED'S COUNTERFEIT FIANCÉE

(Silhouette Desire #1654)

When debonair attorney Jared Westmoreland needed a date, he immediately thought of the beautiful Dana Rollins. Reluctantly, Dana fulfilled his request, and the two were somehow stuck pretending that they were engaged! With the passion quickly rising between them, would Jared's faux fiancée turn into the real deal?

Available May 2005 at your favorite retail outlet.

Silhouette Desire®

**Enjoy the launch of Maureen Child's
NEW miniseries**

THREE-WAY WAGER

*The Reilly triplets bet they could go
ninety days without sex. Hmmm.*

The Tempting Mrs. Reilly
by MAUREEN CHILD

(Silhouette Desire #1652)
Available May 2005

Brian Reilly had just made a bet to not
have sex for three months when his
stunningly sexy ex-wife blew into town.
It wasn't long before Tina had him
contemplating giving up his wager
and getting her back. But the tempting
Mrs. Reilly had a reason of her own
for wanting Brian to lose his bet…
to give her a baby!

COMING NEXT MONTH

#1651 AWAKEN THE SENSES—Nalini Singh
Dynasties: The Ashtons
Charlotte Ashton was quiet and shy, but to renowned winemaker
Alexandre Dupre, she was an intriguing challenge. Charlotte's
guarded ways had him wanting to awaken her senses, and pretty
soon Alexandre was too tempting to resist. Yet, Charlotte didn't just
want a fling—she wanted him forever.

#1652 THE TEMPTING MRS. REILLY—Maureen Child
Three-Way Wager
Brian Reilly had just made a bet not to have sex for three months,
when his stunningly sexy ex-wife blew into town. It wasn't long before
Tina had him contemplating giving up his wager and getting her back.
But the tempting Mrs. Reilly had a reason of her own for wanting Brian
to lose his bet…to give her a baby!

#1653 HEART OF THE RAVEN—Susan Crosby
Behind Closed Doors
When private investigator Cassie Miranda was assigned to find a
mysterious baby, she never thought she'd have to help out his
dashingly handsome father. Reclusive businessman Heath Raven
was hardly prepared to become a dad, but Cassie saw a man with a
hardened heart that she was all too willing to soothe.

#1654 JARED'S COUNTERFEIT FIANCÉE—Brenda Jackson
When debonair attorney Jared Westmoreland needed a date, he
immediately thought of the beautiful Dana Rollins. Reluctantly,
Dana fulfilled his request, and the two were somehow stuck pretending
that they were engaged! With the passion quickly rising between them,
would Jared's faux fiancée turn into the real deal?

#1655 ONLY SKIN DEEP—Cathleen Galitz
To put an end to her single status, Lauren Hewett transformed from shy
bookworm into feisty bombshell while her former crush, Travis Banks,
watched with more than passing interest. Travis wasn't exactly looking
to lay his heart on the line but Lauren wasn't interested in an attraction
that was only skin deep….

#1656 BEDROOM SECRETS—Michelle Celmer
Ever since that one time Tyler Douglas had trouble "performing" in
the bedroom, he'd been too terrified to even be in the same room with a
woman. So when he offered to let the beautiful Tina DeLuca stay in his
home, he did all he could to keep her out of his bed. But Ty was more
than Tina would—or could—resist….

SDCNM0405